Originally published in 2018 by
Adrian Bridget

TEXTS THAT SHOULDN'T
BE READ OUT LOUD

Edited by
Christophe Chauvet
Proofread by
Adam Rohan

British Library Cataloguing-in-
Publication Data

A catalogue record for this book
is available from the British Library

ISBN 978-1-9999702-0-8

Designed by
Tomas Laar
Typeset in
Berthold Akzidenz Grotesk
Cormorant
Printed and bound by
Aquatint, London

TEXTS THAT SHOULDN'T BE READ OUT LOUD

With a foreword by
KENNETH GOLDSMITH

Adrian Bridget

FOREWORD

There's an essay by the writer Gilbert Adair that talks about the importance of using proper names and places in a piece of writing. The capital letters, he claims, hook and anchor the eye so much so that he postulates that a piece of writing can be navigated by merely moving from one name to the other—and you'd still get the gist of the piece. Adair was a newspaperman and every newspaperman knows that the next best thing to headlines are bold-faced names.

So what are we to do with a book that, with the exception of one or two pieces is bereft of proper names? We have to develop alternative reading strategies. The texts become endlessly horizontal seas of words that require a different navigation one that—to continue the aquatic metaphor—requires surfing as much as reading, befitting the digital age during which they were constructed. In Adairian terms then, this is a hookless text, resembling the namelessness and anonymously flat spaces of Beckett's late prose as much as it does the rambling excess of the alphanumeric internet.

Bridget's book has as many moves and moods as the internet itself. Comprised of dozens of forms—list poems, dialogues, online chats, journaling, and confessions, but to name a few—It's a Joycean compendium laced with panoplies of emotion. Yet its subject position remains purposely murky. Although one's first impulse is to ascribe the first person voice to the author, one has a sneaking suspicion that this isn't always Adrian's voice. Instead, it feels like the voice of an auteur—and in the twenty-first century, auteurs choose and construct literature in grippingly physical ways, at once celebrating and obscuring the authorial figure. Paradoxically, these result texts are a series of singularities; there is clearly a strong authorial intention here, but one that wields a cursor as powerfully as it does a keyboard. Sensibility permeates these short pieces. Adrian Bridget's is a destabilized individuality, one that mirrors the way we construct meaning—and art—in the digital age. In a time when all voices are available to us, the ability to skillfully construct a multiauthored text by an individual feels not only proper, but completely contemporary.

The title TEXTS THAT SHOULDN'T BE READ OUT LOUD seems to reify this idea. If one were to read these texts aloud, then a singular voice would emerge, compressing the cacophonous babel of voices found within to something unified. Instead, read them silently. Hear all the voices in your head, for they will sound richly different from one another. Bridget's book is not only stellar authorship, but shows us compelling and powerful new ways to constructing texts.

— **Kenneth Goldsmith**

CONTENTS

"*Being does not see itself. Perhaps it listens to itself. It does not stand out, it is not bordered by nothingness: one is never sure of finding it, or finding it solid, when one approaches a centre of being. And if we want to determine man's being, we are never sure of being closer to ourselves if we 'withdraw' into ourselves, if we move toward the centre of the spiral; for often it is in the heart of being that being is errancy. Sometimes, it is in being outside itself that being tests consistencies. Sometimes, too, it is closed in, as it were, on the outside.*"

Gaston Bachelard

NEUE WILDE

It is important that the cutting-off is performed by the subject whose hand is severed. While being mutilated by an external agent affirms the power of the other towards the individual, to mutilate oneself is a proposal of retraction, lessening the amount of skin surface that translates the outside environment into private sensation.

A HAND EVENTUALLY STOPS SHAKING AFTER BEING CUT OFF.

The reasons for this image to recur as an obsession could be varied or none at all. The pleasure that is derived from it, as with any obsession, comes from the strangeness of the obsession, and not from its cause.

ERROR: The flats sat above a restaurant on the ground floor. Because of the smell, the large windows had to be shut by the start of the evening. I was the first one to move into the building. I was on the top floor. There were three floors. Four flats on each floor. The building was completely taken apart on the inside before being renovated, disfigured. The empty flats had their doors wide open to ventilate the paint and

plaster. There was a knock on my door. A young woman held a bottle
of champagne and a couple of plastic cups. I just moved in and I
wanted to introduce myself, I thought we could celebrate. I told her
that I would love to but unfortunately I had plans that evening and I
would be leaving quite soon. She told me it wasn't a problem. It was
really nice to meet you. I closed the door. I stayed in the flat the whole
evening. I kept the lights out and I didn't move.

The more the shape of one hand is conceived, the more we are forced
to experience the structural logic of ordinary ponderable things. When
you start relating parts, especially those of the past year or so, you're
tending towards the need to break the fingers.

    The absence of anything beyond a vague agony has gradually
emerged: an entirely optical monument as it merely is, consisting of
various diameters. An inner, even secret, latency moves through the
landscape of the flats, as though the larger presence perceived is that
of a cliff.

    And what was a body is broken down into endlessness—

    What you do is you push up your tummy muscles when you inhale
and you pull them back when you exhale. You have somebody watching
you to make sure that you use your tummy muscles and nothing else.
You give space to the end of the lungs and when you pull the tummy
muscles in you can expel the old air. Ok. I will move you a little bit
faster. Inhale. And exhale. Inhale and exhale. It's not easy. It's ok. If
you're coughing it's fine. You're not used to this. Go on. Inhale. Exhale.
Ok. Very good. It's ok. Ok. Relax. Relax. Relax. Go back to normal
breathing. Push out the tummy muscles still. Slowly. And pull them
slowly down. Pushing the tummy muscles slowly up. Much slower.
Much slower. Very slowly. You want to relax. You want to get rid of all
the anger. Very slowly. And then you start to speed up. Inhale. Exhale.
Inhale. Exhale. If you get dizzy open your eyes and look at the ceiling.
Don't overdo anything. Just follow the instinct that you have to do it
slower. You don't need to push yourself. And then pause. Deep and

slow. It's not easy after the fast breathing to get into the deep and slow breathing. Much slower. Very slowly. Inhale to the end of your lungs. And exhale. Now getting faster. Go on. And faster. And faster. Very good. Go on. And what will happen will be tingling in your hands, in your feet, and dizziness in your head. THE DOCTOR BEGINS TO SQUEEZE THE SKIN, AND MAGGOTS START TO EMERGE. REPEATING THE PROCESS A NUMBER OF TIMES, THE MAGGOTS ARE THEN PLACED INTO A QUICKLY FILLING UP DISH, WHERE THEY ARE SEEN TO BE WRIGGLING AROUND.

Cut to:

[NOISE, IN ANALOG VIDEO AND TELEVISION, IS A RANDOM DOT PIXEL PATTERN OF STATIC DISPLAYED WHEN NO TRANSMISSION SIGNAL IS OBTAINED BY THE ANTENNA RECEIVER OF TELEVISION SETS AND OTHER DISPLAY DEVICES. THE RANDOM PATTERN SUPERIMPOSED ON THE PICTURE, VISIBLE AS A RANDOM FLICKER OF "DOTS" OR "SNOW", IS THE RESULT OF ELECTRONIC NOISE AND RADIATED ELECTROMAGNETIC NOISE ACCIDENTALLY PICKED UP BY THE ANTENNA. THIS EFFECT IS MOST COMMONLY SEEN WITH ANALOG TV SETS OR BLANK VHS TAPES. THERE ARE MANY SOURCES OF ELECTROMAGNETIC NOISE WHICH CAUSE THE CHARACTERISTIC DISPLAY PATTERNS OF STATIC. ATMOSPHERIC SOURCES OF NOISE ARE THE MOST UBIQUITOUS, AND INCLUDE ELECTROMAG-NETIC SIGNALS PROMPTED BY COSMIC MICROWAVE BACKGROUND RADIATION, OR MORE LOCALISED RADIO WAVE NOISE FROM NEARBY ELECTRONIC DEVICES. THE DISPLAY DEVICE ITSELF IS ALSO A SOURCE OF NOISE, DUE IN PART TO THERMAL NOISE PRODUCED BY THE INNER ELECTRONICS. MOST OF THIS NOISE COMES FROM THE FIRST TRANSISTOR THE ANTENNA IS ATTACHED TO. DUE TO THE ALGORITHMIC FUNCTIONING OF A DIGITAL

TELEVISION SET'S ELECTRONIC CIRCUITRY AND THE
INHERENT QUANTIZATION OF ITS SCREEN, THE "SNOW"
SEEN ON DIGITAL TV IS LESS RANDOM. MOST MODERN
TELEVISIONS AUTOMATICALLY CHANGE TO A BLUE
SCREEN OR TURN TO STANDBY AFTER SOME TIME IF
STATIC IS PRESENT.]

ERROR: *And going up the stairs it takes so little time to forget where you live, to stop recognizing the numbers on the doors, and all that, still, I keep going up, without knowing on which door to stop, no steps left, and I freeze in front of the last door, holding keys which I know aren't right for that door, or any other door in the building.*

NON-FICTION

at the age of four A drew on a white wall with coloured crayons and G asked A to clean it then G pushed A's head against the wall and told A to use his tongue:

The couch in the living room was blue velvet. A lied on the couch with his face pressed against the back rest. He scratched his face against the velvet with small movements of the head. He had his back turned to B, gigantic and ever-growing, who stood facing the couch. B enjoyed the dark blues of the velvet: A's body cut across the blue. A pretended to sleep.

Ships in the harbour were being smashed together against the harbour wall, until all that could be seen were pieces of wood floating on the water, jumbled with cargoes and bodies. The stricken ships were watched by helpers on the quay and shore who proffered ropes to pull the drowning men to dry land.

B fucks A and A shits on B:

The asphalt was wet. The tops of the cars were wet. A looked outside as no other cars or pedestrians passed by, arranging an imaginary index of possible deviations. He turned the lights on in the living room. It was darker than back home. The smell of mould seeped through the room regardless of the flower motifs on the carpet, of the wooden furniture. There were lampshades, painkillers. D's voice had grown faint. D was just a voice.

The telephone rang.

In the event of a conversation between two people, a lot can be grasped from the volume of the voices taking part in the conversation. To be greeted by a loud voice: the speaker raises his voice to smash the intimacy of the exchange without reaching the emotional investment of a scream. Raising the voice in such a way, the speaker makes public the fact that a conversation is taking place. The physiological need for a comfortable hearing experience ensures the right amount of distance between the bodies of the speakers. The actual existence of a public or audience is irrelevant. It is the mere inference of third party listeners that sets the speakers apart. Rather than being heard, the speakers want to be apart.

The telephone stopped ringing.

B fell asleep.

on the telephone C says when I opened the door I didn't know she was already dead and the hospital bed faced the door and I opened the door and saw her so ugly the eyes were still open and the mouth was open and she wasn't a person anymore from all that bleeding through the pores over the past months you don't know how much I cried today I cried a lot at noon and I don't want to:

The route has been calculated, please drive onto a digitalised road.

The loneliness of C. She made her way through the large shops that sit in isolated warehouses through the countryside, looking for potential purchases: the denim trousers she needed, she absolutely needed, since she had given away the short skirts. There were garments that didn't look her age. She bought the trousers, and carried them back into her car, in a plastic bag.

There was gentle putrefaction.

There was the sound of cars driving safely along the main road.

The flat itself was silent: the sound of cars resonated through the flat at irregular intervals. A sat on the couch listening to the cars go by, his hands resting with their palms up on each side of his body. B would come home anytime now. B had blonde hair. The hair was soft and too long around the ears. No scissors had been put to the lovely hair that curled about his brows, above his ears, longer still on the neck. He wore an English sailor suit, with quilted sleeves that narrowed round the delicate wrists of his long and slender though still childish hands.

A smiled, holding the phone between his right ear and shoulder. He picked a scab on his left shin until it started to bleed. A said, "sorry I couldn't hear the last thing you said." C said, "he called me. I didn't call him. He called me." A said, "oh really? And what did he say?" C said, "he said he'd had some breakthroughs with his family." A said, "was that it?" C said, "that was it." A said, "at least you're still in touch." C said, "I'm not calling him anymore." A said, "I think that's for the best." C said, "I miss you." A said, "we can't do anything about it." C said, "I know." A said, "Let's continue talking tomorrow then." A put the phone down.

The phone rang.

C said, "I knew there was something I was forgetting to tell you about."

B asks A not to forget to start taking the sleeping pills and B takes a couple of them himself even though he doesn't need them but he tells A that if A is going to take them he wants to take them too and A stares at the bottle of pills:

The sprouting potatoes looked like sea creatures: the need to run the fuck away before the smell of the parts of the sea that meet the sewage system would come towards him. The air was heavy enough for the smell to hang low and grip onto it and make its way forward, and then penetrate into all his belongings, and books, and little things that he brought with him because he cherished them.

no sleep and we're sorry to say that and two cigarettes waiting for E to send a message then a picture then E goes back to the hospital no sleep and we're sorry to say that and A smokes two cigarettes and A sits alone in the kitchen in the middle of the night and A falls asleep before E is prescribed antibiotics:

A came home from his sales clerk job. He had been repeating the same three sentences all day. Would you like a bag; the card reader is on your left; thank you have a lovely day. At work, he tied a rubber band around his hand under the counter, occasionally using his thumb to make it tighter.

When it would be morning again, A would have a glass of tap water. He would fold the blankets into perfect squares, smoothing out any creases. A would make the bed. He would make the bed because B liked to see a made bed. A would fold the white t-shirts that were left on the hanger to dry five days ago. He would place the folded t-shirts in a pile on top of the made bed. He would finish doing the dishes. He would get the old sheets from the laundry pile and put them in the washing machine. He would set a short cycle with warm water. He would take the books off the shelves. He would arrange them in separate piles on the floor. He would place the books back on the shelves in the same order as they had been before.

A alternated cigarettes and throat relief pastilles.

There were childhood memories. G coughed covering his mouth with his hand. A looked at his hand before wiping it on his trousers.

A called D. It rang for a long time. The call went to voicemail.

There was a message from E. She was out but she would definitely call him when it would be morning again.

I'm sorry I haven't been calling lately. It's not that I can't actually speak. There is absolutely nothing wrong with my ability to speak. I just can't seem to go beyond the intention. I know what I want to say. I know how I want to say it. I can make myself ready to speak, position myself, open the throat, gather some air. But when the moment comes, I can't *get myself to speak.* / Remembering a phone call that took place earlier today in which I described an imagined phone call to my mother (if I listened to the words of my mouth, I might say that someone else was speaking out of my mouth): so you know about Ferdinand the bull right? I'm pretty sure I told you about it. It's an old Disney short animation, I used to watch it all the time when I was a kid. My mum used to read the story out to me as well. Do you know it? It's a bull that doesn't like fighting and all he wants to do is to smell the flowers. Yeah. So I kept imaging this situation in which I call my mum and then I could hear myself in my head telling her "mum, I travelled the world and left everyone behind so I could smell the flowers but the flowers died in my hand and I don't know what to do now." / I'd rather be outside even if it rains. / As you've asked me, I'm just sending a reminder that I'd prefer working two days a week instead of three. I want to avoid falling ill again due to exhaustion and having to cancel a shift like last week. / You tell me I'm distant and you don't really know how to explain it there are no concrete examples you just feel a distance there all the time: and I SAY: I'm doing the best I can: I'm trying to please everyone: I'm fighting with all my strength every single day just to stop. / In the gallery walls you could see the devotion of the photographer, how he'd devoted himself to just one thing all his life, and because of that he has managed to develop this astounding level of intimacy, and that's so palpable, the intimacy brought by the hours and the time (two discontinuous bodies need to establish an in between space, and maintain this space, so the intimacy can be brought by time and be KEPT in this made up space). I WANT THAT INTIMACY. / You tell me I'm distant and I make you less happy.

F says anything that reminds him of the isolation he felt at the time makes him sick and A says that he understands he's never felt as isolated as he feels now and A sends F a long sequence of messages to which F doesn't reply:

A blew his nose and counted to ten. C taught him to pray as a child, on his knees. He counted to ten. He thought about how whatever his hands made lacked some sort of density that other things, real things, seemed to have. Only sweeping motions. Keep missing you.

A washed his hands before grabbing the phone to tell C he loved her. He used antibacterial soap. He opened the tap. He got a little bit of water on his hands to get the soap to foam. He scrubbed each of the ten fingers individually, then the backs of the hands, the palms. Then the wrists. Forearms. He rinsed the soap. He brought some water to his mouth, spitting it out almost immediately. He closed the tap with the tips of the fingers, trying to touch it as little as possible. He grabbed a white towel with both hands and pressed it against his face.

He called everyone he intended to meet in the coming days. He cancelled all meetings. It didn't make him feel a thing.

B tells A that the smell of cigarettes stays on the insides and A hides in the bedroom and listens to the sound of a knife successively scratching the glass chopping board echoing through the flat while B chops vegetables in the kitchen:

A loved when B said, "it's okay." He crawled under the desk in the smaller bedroom, squeezing to fit in between its legs. His knees were pressed against his chest. He waited. B was in another room. He listened to B tidying the other room as if nothing had changed. A enjoyed listening to B when B didn't know A had crawled under the desk. A didn't move at all. He cherished anticipating the moment when B would find him. He let the thought move around his head. B turned on the lights of the smaller bedroom. "What are you doing there?" A didn't reply. "You can't just stay there like that." B dragged the furniture around the room to free enough space in front of the desk. A enjoyed listening to B when B dragged the furniture around: the clothing hanger, the bookshelf, and the chair. B crouched down on the floor in front of A. B talked to A without making eye contact. "Come on now." B grabbed A by the wrists and pulled him upwards. A loved B. The sound of a car horn broke through the flat. It lasted for ten consecutive seconds.

A heard the sound of someone's voice.

A opened the bedroom door, and listened to B's breathing in complete darkness. B was sleeping.

Delete all messages.

on the telephone A tells C he doesn't look at pictures or old cards or anything like that anymore because people are just too concerned with telling their own life story back to themselves so they can exist and C says she thinks she understands and A thinks about how C can only listen to herself playing the piano and B is about to fall asleep and C says I love you and A comes off the phone briefly and B says I hate it when you leave me:

A couldn't be fucked anymore. His asshole was always bleeding. It made B's balls hurt. And it made B cry at night. B stopped crying. He shouted at A and told A he was worth nothing. A had left everyone he'd ever known because he was a worthless person with a worthless asshole. A stopped picking up the phone. He set it to silent and watched as it would ring without making any noise until it stopped.

A had met E a while back when A thought he would be something special. E thought A would be something special. They were best friends until A made her cry and hate absolutely everything about herself.

E starts to lose her hair and C loses her voice and B falls asleep on the couch and A falls asleep on the couch and A wakes up with a scratching noise coming from inside the wall then B wakes up to find A standing in the middle of the room:

A lives in a foreign country. A speaks in a foreign language. He left home a while back when he thought he would be something special. A is nobody. A works long hours to get by on minimum wage.

A doesn't fuck B because A is too tired to fuck B.

A smokes in a parking lot.

Seething with aggression and sensing the imminent chaos.

That's all.

A cries eating toast with strawberry jam at 3:45am and D says thank you that's a beautiful image:

The kitchen floor was wet. A turned his phone's torch on. The water reflected the light that had come from the torch. He tried to figure out where the water had come from. The cupboards were dry. The counter was dry. There were no leaks coming from the washing machine. It was a small, shallow, puddle of water.

(As I am sitting down, with cold legs, I wonder what are the nauseous lights that blink in the distance. And then stop.)

LANDSCAPE

<< YOU HAVE ONE NEW VOICE MESSAGE >> close your eyes... moving really fast... distorted awareness and little feeling... or you close your eyes and you see something... moving really fast and... so small... what is it... you say you're not sure... did you touch it before... can you touch it now... and you say you're afraid... and then you pretend there's nothing wrong and that is the way people normally look at things... can you touch it now... and you say you're afraid... maybe you just need some gloves to protect your hands while you... what is it... and you ask where can I find gloves... but the gloves just appear... and you say the gloves are not appearing... and you say they're not appearing... maybe thick leather gloves... and you say they're not appearing... and at this point you're quite desperate screaming I can't make the gloves appear... don't touch me like that... and you don't want to touch it... does it hurt... and you say around me... just around me like a second skin

<< YOU HAVE ONE NEW VOICE MESSAGE >> and it doesn't feel real and then the little voice grows and suddenly the little voice got big and all there is is a little voice that tells you things like... do you understand what you see... and what if you don't understand... moving really fast... is there somebody there... are you willing to find out for yourself what's really there in the landscape... when you lied in bed by his side two nights in a row... and it doesn't feel real and then the little voice grows and suddenly the little voice got big and all there is is a little voice in your head going... isn't that so... don't touch me like that... and what if you don't understand what you see... does it hurt... does it hurt while you wait for something remarkable on him... by the sea... moving really fast... two nights in a row... can you touch it now

(and nothing besides a sharp horizon line, we see green, the coast on the foreground, both bleak and vibrant, the bottom quarter divided into three horizontal sections of similar size, the distant sea, the low tide, and the sand, respectively, we see the calm waves, from black to blue and dark browns and strong lines, as it reaches the top right side, light accents bring thicker clouds, both bleak and vibrant, the distant sea, the low tide, and the sand, respectively, dissolve into a bluer shade, as it goes from the left hand side to the right hand side, the sea approaches, a dense formation of light grey, the calm waves that approach, a sky deep and flamboyant opens the picture, three horizontal sections of similar size distinguish the sky from the coast, bleak yellow staining the dark sky, distinguishable from the water only by the use of light browns, and greens, and beige, excessive, light browns, and greens, and beige)

<< YOU HAVE ONE NEW VOICE MESSAGE >> is that what you're feeling now... looking down... kneeling down... wanting him for two nights in a row... and it ends in a very... it's like slamming the breaks on... there's the odd bit of dust floating in front of you... and you

<< YOU HAVE ONE NEW VOICE MESSAGE >> at this point you're quite desperate screaming I can't make the gloves appear... (*laughs*)... it starts like a little voice

(as it goes, from the left hand side to the right hand side, the sky folds into itself, irregular, and nothing besides a sharp horizon line to depict the legs, we see a subtle foreshortening, worked through the calm waves that approach, the lower part of the breast, the torso, the groin, and the upper part of the legs, behind the clouds, as if evening would be approaching, a solid dark brown on the top left hand corner prepares us for orange accents on the lower clouds, distinguishable from the water only by the bottom quarter divided into three horizontal sections of similar size, the distant sea, the low tide, and the sand, respectively, dissolving into light reds and purples, as if evening would be approaching)

<< YOU HAVE ONE NEW VOICE MESSAGE >> I'm waiting for you to pick up the phone... the little voice grows and... pick up the phone... is that what you're feeling now... are you kneeling down... and you say you're afraid... maybe you just need some gloves to protect your hands while you... moving really fast... what is it... and you ask where can I find the gloves

<< YOU HAVE ONE NEW VOICE MESSAGE >> when you lied next to him... two nights in a row... do you understand what you see... is there somebody there... did you touch it before... would he look the same inside... can you touch it now

(the distant sea, the low tide, and the sand, respectively, just above the bellybutton, the upper body starts at the top right hand side, distinguishable from the water only by the use of light browns, and greens, and beige, and nothing besides a sharp horizon line, we see the lower part of the breast, as it goes, the torso, as it goes, the groin, as it goes, and the upper part of legs encounters, in a single line of shadow, the white brushstrokes that might depict a draped bed sheet, or the inside of a garment which is being removed, its perspective worked through a subtle foreshortening of the picture, the bottom quarter divided into three horizontal sections of similar size, the clouds are both light as they are excessive, and at times transparent on the lower part of the breast, with a predominance of pale rose tones, and dark browns, accents of lighter grey are used to depict the calm waves that approach, contrasting the deep black)

<< YOU HAVE ONE NEW VOICE MESSAGE >> does it hurt... you say around me... you don't want to touch it... kneeling down... and scream really loud sounds... when you close your eyes to let his voice move far away and it doesn't matter how far as long as it is far... maybe thick leather gloves... and you say around me... just around me like a second skin... and at this point you're quite desperate screaming I can't make the gloves appear... memories now experienced with distorted awareness and little feeling... moving really fast... and at this point you're quite desperate screaming I can't make the gloves appear

<< YOU HAVE ONE NEW VOICE MESSAGE >> (...)

(there is a gentle arch of shadows just above the bellybutton, in a dense formation of light grey clouds, that gradually descends into greener shades to open up and spread legs, and the hair which is the darkest area, and nothing besides a sharp horizon line, that lasts until the bellybutton nears the distant sea, as it goes, the low tide, as it goes, and the sand, as it goes, respectively)

<< YOU HAVE ONE NEW VOICE MESSAGE >> does it hurt... when you pick up the phone and listen

<< YOU HAVE ONE NEW VOICE MESSAGE >> maybe you just need gloves to protect your hands... the hands shake so much... two nights in

a row... and at this point you're quite desperate... it doesn't feel real... the little voice grows and... don't touch me like that... is that what you're feeling now... and you ask where can I find the gloves but the gloves just appear I'm dying and you say the gloves are not appearing... when you shut the front door for the last time... it's like slamming the breaks on... a pile of sand bags leaning against the door

I saw something shining in the clear blue sky I wondered what it was so I stared at it as the light grew as well as the strange yellow ray there was a flash it exploded right in front of my eyes there was a tremendous noise when all the buildings around me collapsed I didn't even hear any sound the dust was rising and something sandy and slimy entered my mouth I couldn't figure out what it was since I couldn't move or see I couldn't see anything in the dark I covered my eyes and ears with my hands like this the window glass was blown off and I started to count people kept yelling give me water a sea of dead people there wasn't space for the water just people lying there dead my hair was so stiff with dust and we kept running I reached home and of course home was gone and I couldn't find anybody bright red orange red that's what it was like I wondered why there was blood all over her and one of her teeth was missing although she had been in the kitchen all the time her blood spurted out so hard it reached me in the bathroom everything started falling down people looked like ghosts trying to walk before collapsing that's when we saw there was nothing left the engine was so lively I just heard it then we heard the noise fade suddenly there was a moment of blinding light with intense heat I couldn't see anything there was a noise that's impossible to describe followed by a bang the window broke with a bang the sky was always dark and we never knew what time it was all I could see was a broken ceiling and through it the grey sky there seemed to be something dripping from my fingertips a school girl with her eye hanging out of its socket a man clutching a hole in his stomach trying to stop his organs from spilling out I saw that a streetcar had stopped just at that moment and the people still standing dead then something wet started coming down

— (on the telephone) if you were to sleep

  — yes

  — just pretend you are

  — I am thinking of you

  — you are thinking of me

  — smoking

  — to calm yourself down

  — yes

  — if you were to sleep

  — I need something that will distract me from the fact that I'm falling asleep like there's something watching over me

  — I'm here now slowly begin counting out loud backwards starting with the number one hundred saying the words deeper relaxed

  — one hundred deeper relaxed

  — that's good

  — ninety-nine deeper relaxed

  — that's fine

  — ninety-eight deeper relaxed

  — you can let those numbers grow dim and distant

  — ninety-seven deeper relaxed

  — they're not important

  — ninety six

Pause.

  — deeper

Pause.

I DON'T QUITE BELIEVE ANYTHING HAS HAPPENED THOUGH I WATCHED THE WINDOWS BEING SHUT WITH WOODEN BOARDS / MAIN ROADS NO LONGER PASS THROUGH TOWNS BUT LONG-DISTANCE FLIGHTS AND THEIR BODIES SHALL LIE IN THE STREETS OF THE EXCITING NEW CITY / RIG UP ONE ROOM IN YOUR HOUSE AS A REFUGE ROOM A SMALL ROOM AND GIVE ALL THE PROTECTION YOU CAN MAKE IT COMFORTABLE YOU MIGHT

HAVE TO STAY IN IT FOR A LONG TIME / THE BEST PLACE
IS FARTHEST AWAY FROM THE ROOF AND OUTSIDE WALLS
/ WHAT IS STRIKING IS THE UNREALITY OF THE SITUA-
TION I FEEL NO DIFFERENT BUT SUDDENLY IT CANNOT BE
SEEN OR FELT / IT'S A BRIGHT SUNNY MORNING FULL OF
LIFE / TO PROTECT A WINDOW FIX AN OLD DOOR FIRM-
LY ACROSS THE LOWER HALF INSIDE AND OUTSIDE FIRST
REMOVING THE GLASS AND FILL THE INTERVENING SPACE
WITH EARTH / YOU MUST NOT GO OUTSIDE UNTIL IT'S
ABSOLUTELY SAFE YOU WILL NEVER BE ABLE TO JUDGE IT
FOR YOURSELF ADVICE WILL BE GIVEN SO KEEP LISTENING
/ YOU WILL NEED DRINKING WATER FOOD MOSTLY IN TINS
PORTABLE RADIO AND SPARE BATTERIES TIN OPENER AND
BOTTLE OPENER CUTLERY AND CROCKERY WARM CLOTH-
ING BEDDING SLEEPING BAGS PORTABLE STOVE AND FUEL
SAUCEPANS FOR BOILING WATER AND COOKING TORCHES
WITH SPARE BULBS AND BATTERIES CANDLES MATCHES
TABLE AND CHAIRS TOILET ARTICLES SOAP TOILET ROLLS
CHANGE OF CLOTHING FIRST AID KIT HOUSEHOLD
MEDICINES AND PRESCRIBED MEDICINES BOX OF SAND
CLOTHS AND TISSUES FOR WIPING PANS AND UTENSILS
NOTEBOOK AND PENCIL FOR MESSAGES BRUSHES SHOVEL
CLEANING MATERIALS RUBBER OR PLASTIC GLOVES TOYS
BOOKS AND MAGAZINES

FUR

<fur1.jpg> to the imaginary over the real / but this place / that swells and shrinks / as we speak

<fur2.jpg> and these forces are so sudden / sometimes below the singing voice / emit sounds that must be called, in / the fine points of their movement

<fur3.jpg> by reviving / the very human will for calm / the experience of all those who / end as our breath ends

<fur4.jpg> thus appears / with astonishing exactness / the breath that is / the imaginary life

<fur5.jpg> the whole group of oral and respiratory conditions / shouting, whispering, intoning / will penetrate and live / much too angular

<fur6.jpg> light, we will / by such total submission / understand how different this is / then there begins a silence

<fur7.jpg> slows down / on its proper sound value / a complete psychology of air / in a throat that is rich in nerve endings

<fur8.jpg> still they are / echoes and resonances / artificial and tainted / let us make no noise

<fur9.jpg> when this silence has fallen / between the universe and the breather / then the lips gently separate and seem to aspire the air

<fur10.jpg> if we were to soothe / all the tumult within us: / in aerial imagination / a day whose rhythm is / only shallow breaths

LDN

I sit down WITH SHAVED HEAD, LOOKING OVER LEFT SHOULDER. MOVE FROM THE AUTOBIOGRAPHICAL TO AUTOBIOGRAPHY; WRITE TEXT "NOTES" USING ALL CAPITALS; IT FEELS AS IF NOTHING HAS TAKEN PLACE IN THE PAST THREE YEARS; LAUGHING AT HOW JUVENILE THOSE DRAWN OUT SEPARATIONS BETWEEN INNER AND OUTER WORLDS NOW SEEM; "PLEASE SIT DOWN AND SMILE AND STAY STILL WHILE I SLOWLY CUT YOUR CLOTHES OFF BEFORE FINALLY STARING AT YOUR BODY THEN FORCING MY HEAD ONTO YOUR ABDOMEN WITH MY ARMS AROUND YOU AND THEN I WILL SWIM."

    [A room on the ground floor with windows facing a street in any large city where it's cold and cloudy on a Wednesday late afternoon; six tables; a single person on each table; they stare straight ahead in silence right through the modest flower arrangements. One dies: there's a free seat by the window. Two people sit down. (smoking). An exercise repeated two times in the morning and two times in the evening.

They sit down facing each other and take turns saying "you-are-so-beautiful." The duration of each practice varies. It should, however, progressively wane towards mutual silence. And then again.]

(lights down)

The cab driver screamed, turned to face the back seat where he sat, he looked at him, he screamed again, his eyes blank and his eyes blank, fleshed himself beyond recognition, he closed his eyes, the cab driver reached for his hand, both fell in and out of love, forget my address. Open the door. He crawled onto the pavement, still wet, with his hands, right, left. I want to watch you drive away.

(lights up)

And you see that particular kind of straight line that divides the building and the sky.

Push the glass panel of the revolving door: enter the lobby: high ceiling / very little furniture / a red chair in a small corner / small glass table by your side / nothing on top of the small round glass table / marble floors. The back wall is made entirely of glass. There is nothing to be seen on the other side. There was no one else there. I was waiting for the lift. I felt it as it came and blest the giver of oblivion.

A man leans naked against the kitchen counter. He spreads his butt cheeks apart and tells an unknown man jerking off by the door to come and fuck his ass. He grabs an empty coke glass bottle and inserts it into his asshole just up to the point the bottle starts getting larger. He plays with it for a while. The unknown man approaches him. He puts the bottle back on the kitchen counter. The unknown man pulls his trousers down and his jumper up just about enough to be comfortable. Without taking off the sunglasses, the unknown man spits on his cock and shoves it inside his ass. The unknown man fucks him holding onto his shoulder. He keeps spreading his butt cheeks apart. There is another man sitting at the kitchen table playing with his phone while he gets fucked. He asks if the tightness feels good. The unknown man that is fucking him says yes. The unknown man comes inside his ass. The unknown man pulls his cock out. Cum drips down his balls. The unknown man puts his cock in again and fucks him a little more, then pulls it out again. He walks towards another man who is jerking off on the living room couch. He climbs on the couch and sits on his cock. They fuck. Another man watches them fucking. The doorbell rings and they stop. Information is encoded, stored, retrieved, and corrupted.

A new season arrives with images of other seasons that have come before. I did not know what these pictures were. The seasons had grown. The lift opened with the announcement of the "Fourteenth Floor". I thought all I had to do was turn around and walk away and it would all be over. His office was behind the last door on the right in a succession of unidentified doors in the corridor of the fourteenth floor. He lit up my cigarette, saying nothing. I told him that yes, it was really what I wanted, to be here.

I've never heard your voice.

Through the sound system: hear the conductor's heavy breathing. The lights flickered. All passengers remain silent, isolated. Heads down and dim. A man and a man sat across from each other. Inhale: through the sound system: exhale: the lights flickered. They got in the train and it doesn't matter where they are going now as long as they keep going on and: through the sound system: heavy breathing. They keep going. I suffer the prospect of meeting you. The train approaches the next stop.

The doors open and without warning he drags him out of the train and keeps running through the station through the parking lot through the middle of the night. It's cold.

I found myself regretting the room and the way I breathe inside the room. There were no faces allowed, or wanted. The suppression of all personality traits, as expected, as rehearsed many times before, in front of mirrors and at pedestrian crossings, in front of glass sheets. Even the most simple of actions is an injury, for even the most simple of actions implies a mark, a trace. Residue.

[Keep an eye out for anyone coming through the door with a knife, I
don't want to get my throat cut. An exercise repeated two times in the
morning and two times in the evening. They sat for a long time. Both of
them were too uncomfortable to ask the waiter if their order had been
forgotten. He sat with his back to the restaurant's door. He sat FACING
HIM. He thought he would have had his big break by now. He wondered
quite frequently if it had been presumptuous of him to have thought he
was actually worth something. MAYBE he hasn't been sleeping again.
He considered, for a long time, if he should reach out and touch his hand.
He wasn't really listening. IF HE HAD BEEN listening he would have
known that he felt like he didn't exist because no one would return his
emails phone calls messages etc. He loved him because he didn't exist.]

I have to destroy everything I make.

It took a long time to realize. And I'm sorry for everything that
it's put you through. I know it wasn't what you expected. I know you
have time after time encountered in me this sort of pulling away, or a
tight muscle. And there can be no suspicion about the authenticity of
what is being shown: this sort of pulling away.

I let my index finger make an easy pendulum movement of small
amplitude. A touch was still painful yesterday. I am leaving the room
because you tell me to. Someone leads you by the hand, sometimes left,
sometimes right. What makes an image of him into an image of him
though it was only his finger in the air? Be ready for the tug of his hand.
For the same purpose move the hand of a clock till its position strikes
me. In what sense is it true that my hand does not feel pain? When I
touch the object I look not at my hand.

"The classic way of starting is by making a Y shaped incision starting
on the chest and then extending to the pubic area the ribs are being cut
you see the heart and lungs in place the heart has been removed remove
the lungs free up all the tissues so that the neck can be removed with
the tongue now reflecting the scalp reach down into the optical nerves
and there's another cut": couldn't believe the man I'd fantasize to fuck

me on top of the desk of the man who was actually fucking me. Silent ejaculation followed by convulsive tearing of the sterile eyes. Several changes of day and night passed, and the orb of the night had greatly lessened, when I began to distinguish my sensations from each other.

He left: looking at the empty chair across the office desk: getting heavier: maybe three hours. I expect the smoke to come slowly out of my open mouth and forget, inebriated, forget the adding up of skin on top of skin (menthol-flavoured bone cells rising up and erasing themselves on the top of my head), BREATHE IN, the two lungs now syncopated and *b l a c k o u t*

the

the

the eyes

the eyes which keep switching,

the eyes which keep switching, on and off

the eyes which keep switching, on and off, we are in maybe a park there's a lot of grass and it feels like we can't lie down anywhere now because the grass is just so green and it's all just so wide and spread out and if we lie down we might lose ourselves on the grass that doesn't start nor end blurring the distances we allowed ourselves so we keep walking even though there are tired legs inside our walking legs so tired you hit me on the back of the head with a large stone and I fall down on the grass while you watch me, standing, you light up a cigarette, you applaud me and I fall asleep.

I opened the door, just enough to talk through it.

I whispered through the gap.

I remember now.

The uncouth and inarticulate sounds which broke from me frightened me into silence.

He grabs me in his arms. He takes me outside and puts me down on the large grass area at the back of the building. I think I'm drooling and cannot control it. There's water coming out of my mouth. He washes his hands.

And it was not without discomfort that he sat next to a mirror, under the observation of subjects ONE and TWO, who'd take notes. TWO unties his shoelaces. ONE says, "would you please tie your laces?" He leans down to do as he was told. ONE and TWO take notes. He starts to tie the shoelaces as he had done numerous times since learning it for the first time, trusting his fingers enough to pay them no attention in each subsequent time. If the situation were otherwise he'd probably chuckle at the thought of not actually remembering most of the times he had tied up his shoelaces. The fingers now don't seem to know how to hold them. ONE and TWO take notes. "Thank you, you can stop now." He brings his torso back up. TWO grabs him by the arms, lifting him to a standing position. TWO says, "would you please walk in a straight line till the end of the room and then walk back?" His shoelaces are still loose. He starts walking. He can't see the edge of the room. Bright white without lines or corners. The mirror frames an image of his backside, which doesn't move for a long time before falling out of sight.

CLAUSTROPHOBIA

RE: claustrophobia:
you were panting last night I woke up in the middle of the night and
you were panting and I've been meaning to ask you why you were
panting but I didn't feel like that was the right thing to do I went
back to sleep and we woke up in the morning we talked and we talked
differently than we usually do because for you nothing had changed but
for me I knew you had been panting in your sleep and I tried to pretend
that I hadn't heard you panting but to be perfectly honest I can still
hear and see you panting in your sleep like I did last night I can still
feel the way I felt when I heard and saw you panting in your sleep and
I should ask you why you were panting in your sleep but then (a) you
might not remember you were panting and you might feel embarrassed
to have been panting unconsciously or (b) you might remember you
were panting in your sleep and you might be completely unembar-
rassed and that would break me because I would think I don't know
you as well as I think I do because in the way I know you you would
be embarrassed by the fact you were panting last night or even (c) you

might be embarrassed and I might be happy to know you were embarrassed just like I thought you would be but then you would explain why you were panting last night and the reason might be something that I'd rather not know I'll have your panting muffled in the back of my head every time I look at you and as the years go by I will get used to the panting I will grow to find it tender and whenever I will not hear the panting I will miss it and I might ask you to sit in front of me and be quiet just so I can look at you and hear the panting again muffled in the back of my head if you would start to talk to me you would break me because I wouldn't be able to hear the panting muffled under your voice or (d) maybe now I should say I have something I've been meaning to ask you and we would laugh at first but when the laughing would subside I would look at you and the back of my head would be absolutely empty

RE: claustrophobia:

A room, white painted walls, timber-framed sash windows, single-glazed, with four panes per sash, recessed timber panels in between the sash windows, timber slatted floor planks in maple, ceiling mounted fluorescent batten lights, twin tube, without diffusers, empty except for three chairs in a random configuration.

The storm. Asleep on the couch. How he had erased the texts on the back of the photographs last night. This room. Three chairs. The discomfort of every person who once sat at a dining table to look up and face whoever sat across them, if any did, and talk.

"I'm sorry. I forgot to ask how was your day." "It was alright." "That's good to hear." "What did you do today?"

It starts somewhere between the forming of an intention and the launch into action, shoes are taken off.

Turn on and off and on and off and on and off the fluorescent tube lights, flickering to phase in the totality of the room, turn the lights on, and wait a few seconds by the door before slowly stepping into the room.

"The principle and first of beings is immoveable both essentially and according to accident: but he moves the first, eternal and single motion. But since that which is moved must necessarily be moved by something, and that which first moves is essentially immoveable, and an eternal motion must be moved by an eternal mover (...) it is necessary that each of these celestial motions should be moved by an essentially immoveable and eternal essence." (Aristotle, Metaphysics, Book XII.)

Flowers. A thought on how the photographs had become less common until they had to stop. Thirty-second birthday. The view from the window. The impossibility of all those things being completely torn as their image recurs.

He walks to the centre of the room, takes off his coat, drapes it onto one of the three chairs as he observes the other two. A chair that looks like himself. He sits down, brings his elbows to his knees, letting his head turn around to look at the white walls and the white pipes that run along the junctions and the windows with opaque glass tiles.

The glass panes of the windows shaking and trembling; the air made its way forcefully through every breach; sound of a single chord.

He finds himself wanting to speak not without first doubting the absurdity of the action until after a few minutes of sitting on the chair, elbows on knees: "okay."

In his hands he holds the face that domestic evenings had stripped of hunger, touching it like mirrors do. The presence of others is elongated into empty rooms, one keeps pacing like one does among people.

He removes his coat from the other chair and lays it on the floor.

HE REARRANGES THE CHAIRS OVER AND OVER AGAIN TRYING TO ESCAPE THE INVISIBLE TRIANGLES THEY TRACE ON THE TIMBER FLOOR.

"Those who are not wrapped in lethargy and who feel vague longings for spiritual life (...) cry in harsh chorus, without any comfort to them. The night of spirit falls more and more darkly. Deeper becomes the misery of these blind and terrified guides, and their followers, tormented and unnerved by fear and doubt, prefer to this gradual darkening the final sudden leap into the blackness." (Kandinsky, 1914)

HE REARRANGES THE CHAIRS OVER AND OVER AGAIN TRYING TO ESCAPE THE INVISIBLE TRIANGLES THEY TRACE ON THE TIMBER FLOOR. He brings the chair that still smells of his coat to the centre of the room, facing the direction of the door. This movement begins in one direction which, after a few seconds, proves to be the wrong one: that is to say, the opposite to that intended. The direction is then changed, after a brief moment of immobility.

He stands with his back to the chair, and lets himself collapse. The impact of his body onto the chair resonates the entirety of his weight.

"I am leaving tomorrow." "Please don't cry." "I'm fine." "Just let me know if you need any help or anything." "Thank you." "I'm off to bed." "I don't feel like sleeping yet." "Wake me up before you leave."

"Good night."

Sitting down, reaching forward with his bare feet, he slides down the chair. The edge of the seat collecting his shirt and scratching the skin on his back. The palms of the hands push against the floor.

The restlessness doesn't subside. Craving that forwardness, beyond the body, the room. The way things happened to turn out. He finds himself wanting to speak not without first doubting the absurdity of the action.

He moves the chairs, will keep doing so, a little faster each time, until the movement patterns that are drawn on the floors succumb to the movement patterns that are drawn in time.

A chair that looks like himself; a chair that smells of his coat; a chair that will remain unknown.

Without moving.

Desire.

Desire.

The storm is unstoppable. Last night is unstoppable. The old house is unstoppable. Flowers are unstoppable. A thought on how the photographs had become less common until they had to stop is unstoppable. Thirty-second birthday is unstoppable. The view from the window is unstoppable.

He finishes taking his shirt off.

The feeling of terror lies in each time he has been moved, has arranged the chairs in a particular configuration inside the room: how each time he has, in fact, lost all the other configurations, the other possible rooms: things not said aloud, a silence that fertilised the invisible things abruptly, the corrosion of a life built ever so carefully with simple movements of the hands: he halts with embarrassment: sudden awareness of the body: a room, white painted walls, timber-framed sash windows, single-glazed, with four panes per sash, recessed timber panels in between the sash windows, timber slatted floor planks in maple, ceiling mounted fluorescent batten lights, twin tube, without diffusers, empty, except for three chairs in a random configuration.

He puts his shirt on.

He ties his shoelaces

He picks his coat up from the timber floor.

He listens to the glass panes in the windows shaking and trembling with the wind. Cacophony.

He meticulously places the chairs back on the same spot in which he had found them.

(He left the room with the lights on, and gently closed the door as to not make any sound.)

RE: claustrophobia:

I hope that this video is somehow 0:07 helpful not actually to me but ███

███████████████████████████████████████

███████████████████████████████████████

███████████████████████████████████████

███████████████████████████████████████

███ *to escape all the things 0:34 that meant it okay for everybody to use 0:37 the fact I suffer 0:42 something to leave me 0:46 with other something with which they 0:48 might you know be compassionate 0:52 I'm now living in a travel lodge motel in* ████████████████
████████████████████ *1:03 just absolutely nobody in my life except 1:06 my doctor my psychiatrist sweetest man 1:10 on hurting that says I'm his hero and that's 1:12 bad the only fucking thing keeping me alive 1:14 at the moment if I'm his bloody hero 1:18 that's kind of pathetic then I gave so 1:21 much love in my life and I just can't 1:26 understand how a person could be left 1:28 alone tonight 1:30 wanted everyone to see what is like* ███████ *1:32 you know* █████████
██
████████████████████████████████ *and suddenly all the people who 1:44 are supposed to be loving you taking 1:46 care of you are treating you like shit 1:48 and then when you're angry or you're 1:51 hurt because they're doing it it's like* ████████████
██

███ *1:58 I'm fighting fighting fighting fighting* ███████████
██

████████ *I love the 2:08 people that are doing this to me 2:10 I'm not staying alive for me if it 2:13 was me I'd be gone* ████████████
██

██

████████████████████ *everyone so afraid and I'm gonna 2:37* ███████████
████████████████████████ *I don't start screaming 2:41 shouting at people I don't you know so a 2:43 big hairy man that must be my family is 2:46 so scared of* ████████████████████████

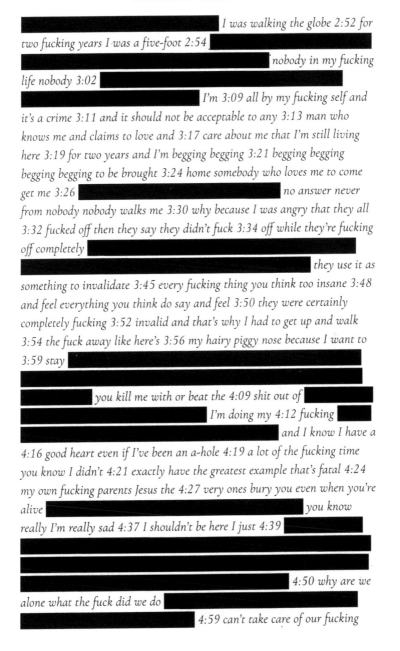

I was walking the globe 2:52 for two fucking years I was a five-foot 2:54 nobody in my fucking life nobody 3:02 I'm 3:09 all by my fucking self and it's a crime 3:11 and it should not be acceptable to any 3:13 man who knows me and claims to love and 3:17 care about me that I'm still living here 3:19 for two years and I'm begging begging 3:21 begging begging begging begging to be brought 3:24 home somebody who loves me to come get me 3:26 no answer never from nobody nobody walks me 3:30 why because I was angry that they all 3:32 fucked off then they say they didn't fuck 3:34 off while they're fucking off completely they use it as something to invalidate 3:45 every fucking thing you think too insane 3:48 and feel everything you think do say and feel 3:50 they were certainly completely fucking 3:52 invalid and that's why I had to get up and walk 3:54 the fuck away like here's 3:56 my hairy piggy nose because I want to 3:59 stay

you kill me with or beat the 4:09 shit out of I'm doing my 4:12 fucking and I know I have a 4:16 good heart even if I've been an a-hole 4:19 a lot of the fucking time you know I didn't 4:21 exactly have the greatest example that's fatal 4:24 my own fucking parents Jesus the 4:27 very ones bury you even when you're alive you know really I'm really sad 4:37 I shouldn't be here I just 4:39

4:50 why are we alone what the fuck did we do 4:59 can't take care of our fucking

*selves idiot 5:03 you gotta take care of us we're all like 5:06 everybody else
we're doing our best* ▮▮▮▮▮▮▮▮▮▮▮▮▮▮▮▮▮

▮▮▮▮▮▮▮▮▮▮▮▮▮▮▮▮▮▮▮▮▮▮

▮▮▮ *bring me home I can't make it home by 5:17 myself like I'm what am I
going home to 5:19 anyway except a whole lot of shit people 5:21 treat me
so bad and what are their 5:23 claims about I end up wishing I was 5:26
dead or clean 5:28 anyway the bunch of assholes jumping on 5:31 me like
I'm a fucking cripple and then 5:33 I'm not allowed to be angry it's like
repeating 5:35 my childhood all over again you know you 5:37 get your face
smashed in and fucking if 5:39 you lift your hand to protect yourself 5:41
they'll tell you you assaulted them it's 5:43 like oh my God* ▮▮▮▮▮▮▮
▮▮▮▮▮▮▮▮▮▮▮▮▮▮▮▮▮ *5:48 I can't get
anywhere and they're not 5:50 even* ▮▮▮▮▮▮▮▮▮▮▮▮▮▮
▮▮▮▮▮▮▮▮▮▮▮▮▮▮▮▮▮▮▮▮▮▮ *and
my entire life 5:59 is revolving around just not dying 6:01 and that's not
living so I'm not going to do 6:05 I'm not gonna die but still this is no 6:08
way for people to be living like* ▮▮▮▮▮▮▮ *every home is breathing
made a 6:13 mystery until insane tell me the same 6:14 story the electricity
between me and them I have a 6:18 fucking apartment which I don't
anymore 6:23 living in the fucking travel lodge 6:25 everybody hello*

▮▮▮▮▮▮▮▮▮▮▮▮▮▮▮▮▮▮▮▮▮▮

▮▮▮▮▮▮▮▮▮▮▮▮ *should not be 6:33 acceptable 6:35 you
don't even care for fuck's sake 6:38* ▮▮▮▮▮▮▮▮▮▮

▮▮▮▮▮▮▮▮▮▮▮▮▮▮▮▮▮▮▮▮▮▮

▮▮▮▮▮▮▮▮▮▮▮▮▮▮▮▮▮▮▮▮▮▮

▮▮▮▮▮▮▮▮▮▮▮▮▮▮▮▮▮▮▮▮▮▮

▮▮▮▮▮▮▮▮▮▮▮▮ *6:56 shit oh fuck back so fucking what
6:58 at the end of the day what is going on I can no one 7:04 could manage
it* ▮▮▮▮▮▮▮▮▮▮▮▮▮▮▮▮▮▮ *7:11 but
not my fucking body remember kitty 7:14 kidney stone unit I was suppose
to survive I was all 7:16 the only person in my life my doctor 7:18 begging
the man to bring me home give me a sofa 7:21 anything so that I'm 7:24
reduced* ▮▮▮▮▮▮▮▮▮▮▮▮▮▮▮▮

███████████████████████████████████

███████████████████████████████████

███████████████████████████████████

███████████████████████████████████

███████████████████████████████████

████████████ *this 7:55 is a fucking joke anyway*

███████████████████████████████████

███████████████████████████████████

███████████████████████████████████

███████████████████████████████████

██████████ *I don't want to die I 8:14 want to stay alive but I want*
to stay 8:16 alive 8:17 ████████████████████████████

███████████████████████████████████

██████████ *and everybody that's fucking 8:26 killing me right now 8:28 it's*
for damn I'm not gonna die but 8:32 anyway I wanted just to meet in there
8:34 that you would all see what the fuck 8:36 it's like you know and
understand like 8:40 ██████████████████████

███████████████████████████████████

███████████████████████████████████

███████████████████████████████████

██████████ *8:59 visit them in the hospital you don't anybody 9:01*
awful but all hello █████████████████████████████

███████████████████████████████████

███████████████████████████████████

███████████████████████████████████ *9:23 strangers*
who are kinder to 9:26 me than my own love song for fuck's sake 9:29 the
stranger on Facebook sending me fucking 9:31 flowers 9:34 for crying out loud
two years solitary confinement 9:38 is enough please will somebody in my
9:42 body act like they give a shit 9:46 where do you think I'm dying a
fucking 9:47 brass country █████████████████████

███████████████████████████████████

██████████████████████████████ *I don't deserve 10:00*

THEATRE

All of these scenes reveal their efforts to suppress the reality of their situation under the formality of theatrical procedures.

[there was a light on]

And all you can see when you shut your eyes is people. *HE rolls over on his side and relapses into sleep.*

[it's very hot].

I cannot see your face. *HE raises his hat.* We move, don't we. I want to hear a warm, thrilling voice cry. That too. Wouldn't it have dried up. Nothing more worth saying. All the singing and smoking. I did not run away from you. Except you. You were all for it earlier on. I mean it sarcastically. The despair and the bitterness. And it doesn't mean anything to you. Manifest nonsense. And tasted the eternal joys of heaven. Forget it. I'm sorry it happened. And I liked doing it with my bare hands. I went to the pictures last week, and some old man was smoking in front, a few rows away. I actually got up, and sat right behind him. What an upsetting thing to see. I have enjoyed, too, my rests, my recuperations,

my breathing times. I'm feeling as I feel now. And there isn't much of
it left. It doesn't matter. Every time you try to escape I will catch you.
Cover your face. Give you good night. You can have the bed. I'll sleep
on the floor. But you haven't answered my question. I said: have you
watched somebody die. What's happening here is a dream. I want to
stand up in your tears, and splash about in them, and sing. I want to
be there when you grovel. I want to be there, I want to watch it, I want
the front seat. I think that's the joy of it. Should have cut my throat.

[a hand in the darkness].

Tell me what that would be. When I saw you standing there
tonight, I knew that it was all utterly wrong. Something you shouldn't
know. But I must on, for back I cannot go. Not for years and years and
years. I'm all right now. I never lose concentration. I never sleep. There
isn't any blood. I cannot conceive you. I must have just lain down in the
snow. I was thinking you might stay a little longer. I noted the gleam
of gold from a dead tooth in the laughing mouth. I must be getting
sentimental. In the harvest of my summer joys. I know it's not all about
excitement. You're hurt because everything has changed. I could stay
here forever. Until it lay splattered all over the lavatory bowl. I guess I
can't help it. You've settled in so easily somehow. I will now go further,
and confess to you that men get tired of everything. That's right. If you
want to make audiences cry, make them laugh at the same thing first.
Now it is all over. So you'd better get some sleep. I can't have one day
and then go back. I'll go on to the end after this. And I don't think I
want to see anyone hurt until I've had something to eat first. You'd have
to stay. I tunnel into the recesses of my mind and I find nothing. *THEY
breathe out and try to smell their own breath.* But if you dwelt in heaven,
as I do, you would realise your advantages. To watch the minutes of this
night. This time in a movie.

[the grass growing through the cracks].

It started during those first months we were alone. Not any more.
It wasn't your fault. I can't sleep. Let it all go. Moves the universe. The
shyness. I'll go out walking. Just one day. That was the idea. If only

something. Sentimental when you repeat it. I didn't know.

[the last bell].

Go easy on it. I became famous for running away from it. I've never seen such hatred in someone's eyes before. I slipped in it. To gracious fortunes of my tender youth. Fingers down throats. Ceremonies matter to us. And back they will come. I might. To see the back of a person disappearing quickly. That damned trumpet. Wait, don't. Not yet. There's nobody but you. I watched you. I'm not saying you can't kill. Maybe you have. And that truth moves me profoundly. I had to convince myself that everything I remembered about this place had really happened to me once. You were away a long time. I did not care. You make beauty and it disappears. Watch the smoke and see it move. Like the games that children play. I remembered them and desperately strove to recover their illusion. It doesn't matter what you believe. I feel it just the same. You'll see in the morning what a beautiful place this is. I'd never know, or you either. When you've just stepped in you can't tell what's going to happen. One sees how things change. Just hold it there. There is something statuesque about it. Your shoulders are very tight. That's why there was so much blood. Too anxious to please. Why don't you do something with it. Passionately and sincerely.

HOTEL

(lying down on the floor and just staying there as long as) JANUARY: He goes up the stairs, gets a key out his pocket. IF YOU HAVE TO WALK ALONE AT NIGHT TAKE EXTRA CARE. I feel like something is going to happen. Lock your doors and windows. I cannot sleep until the sun rises. Make sure your doors are strong and secure. And I think such horrible things. Glass panels on doors are particularly vulnerable. There is nothing here. Something may happen and no one would know and haven't been able to sleep for the past two nights. I have the same strange sense that something is inside with me. He opens the door.

The couch is in the middle of the room, the only piece of furniture, beige, and there are green-leafed plants in **(issuing imaginary letters of apology)** red ceramic pots where the walls meet the floor. She sits on the couch and looks straight at him. He drops his bag next to the couch and hands her the key. "Light-fuck." "Swinging, swinging." "Canine, no glands." "But lots of tongue." "Still dry." "Are you hungry?" "I suppose there's nothing warm." "There's some bread in the closet."

"Same closet?" "It's the door on the right." "I don't like the crust."
"Something to drink?" "You look at me, and I look back at you."
"I understand that." "Turn around." He ate hair soup. He **(that luke-
warm pain and the sheer narcissism)** ate hair soup with no teeth. He
ate hair soup with no teeth, choking. He looked at her. He looked at
the back of her head, bald. He looked around. He talked to make her
cry. He talked about fiction to make her cry. He didn't know her. He
ate her hair. He looked around the room. He kissed her forehead.

No, not at all.

On some days.

On more than half the days.

Nearly every day.

Every night this happened.

There was no quietness until the house was burned.

I LEFT THE KEYS ON THE KITCHEN TABLE / I left the wallet / on
the kitchen table / pictures that were inside the wallet / on the kitchen
table / on the kitchen table / I left the pack / of cigarettes / I left the
jacket / on the kitchen table / I left the trousers / on the kitchen table /
my shirt / on the kitchen table / on the kitchen table / I left my underwear / and shoes / I left / the socks on the kitchen table / on the kitch-
en table / on the kitchen table / I left the fingernails / on the kitchen
table / the lips on the kitchen table / the lips I left the / I left the / I left
the lashes / on the kitchen table / on the kitchen table / I left the eyes /
on the kitchen table / I left my hands / on the kitchen table

FEBRUARY: *Have you found little pleasure or interest in doing things?
Have you found yourself feeling down, depressed or hopeless? Have you had
trouble falling or staying asleep, or sleeping too much? Have you been feeling
tired or had little energy? Have you had a poor appetite or been overeating?
Have you had some trouble concentrating on things like reading the paper
or watching TV? Have you been moving or speaking slowly, or been very
fidgety, so that other people could notice? Have you thought that you'd be*

better off dead or hurting yourself in some way? That's not what they said.
They said before it happened I'd hear a sound, a kind of rumble, and
then I'd know. <<Maybe it develops further, it is still a possibility.>>
I stopped **(on a common dinner in July shaking and trembling)** by the
doorway. *There is a progressive emptying out at the end of fast movements
in a sequence.* Remembrances are mostly constituted of residues of
images that are fictionally overlaid onto actually lived instances.
The children who, isolated from one another, strangers to one another,
started crying precisely **(not a sound)** at the same time. Visual spasms.
Outside of the room, the long corridors may be compared to a **(no
way you could have known with the eyes closed and all)** experience
of divination. On the long corridors on the third floor, with red and
beige patterns on the carpet, this constant trembling. More of it. The
next sentence is a dull sentence. First I need to cover up the bed then
turn off the lights then pretend I really want this. Right here, where
your eyes are looking at now. Like any object that hasn't got any life,
or any coughing, or even the little things like the ants that are crawling
inside the dog's mouth and the dog doesn't move to let the ants move
inside it. You're slipping through the cracks. I undressed. I stopped. "It's
cold in here." "I know." "Is the heating on?" "Yes." **(found the ones who
lock themselves up not without the stink)** "It makes me feel so much
more tired than usual." "Try to keep yourself warm and I'll be back
soon." [note: This conversation has been repeated next door for the last
twenty-seven days at 5pm.] I stared at myself naked in the mirror. The
mirror hangs on the inside of the door. *You have to understand that it
is absolutely normal to experience blackouts.* A chronic fatigue: eyes up.
Down.

Once a day, for the last twenty-seven days, I stared at myself
naked in the mirror always as if it was the first time, leaned forward
and put my right arm against the mirror **(and they're all the same)** as if
it was the first time, forehead against the right arm, reached upwards
with the left hand towards the door frame. Stay there. That's all. So
the body pauses. Reload. A psychological duplication of mastication,

peristalsis, defecation. Every now and then. <<There's nothing I can give you at this stage.>> Sleep comes short, with regular intervals.
once he heard on the radio that there is sound to be found in *2,200 GLORIOUSLY AIR-CONDITIONED ROOMS* the vacuum of outer space *AT THE HOTEL LOCATED DIRECTLY ACROSS THE STREET FROM THE STATION* there are electromagnetic vibrations *EACH OF THE ATTRACTIVE COMFORTABLE GUEST ROOMS* that can now be detected *HAS A CONTINUOUS DEEP RESONANT SOUND PRIVATE BATH CIRCULATING ICE WATER RADIO AND TELEVISION.* "They said before it happened I'd hear a kind of rumble and then I'd know."

ON THE TWENTY-EIGHTH DAY (1): He opened the door of **(not a sound)** the room and looked out **(not a sound)** into the long corridor as **(not a sound)** if it was the first **(not a sound)** time walked to the part **(not a sound)** of the wall that's opposite **(not a sound)** the room door stay there **(not a sound)** down down down sit down **(not a sound)** with his back against the **(not a sound)** part of the wall that's **(not a sound)** opposite the room door no **(not a sound)** clothes on pissed himself watching **(not a sound)** one of the next door **(not a sound)** occupants arriving early in the **(not a sound)** morning still not a sound **(not a sound)** not what they said they **(not a sound)** said he'd hear a kind **(not a sound)** of rumble. He dropped down to the carpet, in the long corridor, as silently as if we were to watch a film of an earthquake with the sound switched off. Thick with the Here Wherein I stood My rested eyes Broke, and searched, a little space. Left untold. I found sighs, not caused by tortures. Then I felt a crash on the bounds of a voice I heard. And others many more. There ceased the sound. Let us on. Let us lose ourselves from whoever can turn round without going that far. As far as I can see it is the same going about looking for pain. Someone plunged in a place in which no one can enter. Come away into the harbour. They will no longer be in the world. ON THE TWENTY-EIGHTH DAY (2): 6.45am, wakes up; 6.50am, makes the bed; 6.55am, walks into the bathroom; 7.00am, brushes teeth with prescription toothpaste; 7.05am, washes the face with unperfumed soap; 7.10 am, takes off underwear; 7.15am, finishes putting on uniform; 7.20am, ties black shoelaces; 7.25am, walks back into the bathroom; 7.30am, finishes fixing the hair; 7.35am, sits by the bed and waits; 7.40am, straightens the bed sheets; 7.45am, walks to the reception desk; 7.50am, checks through a list of occupied rooms; 7.55am, takes the reception phone off the hook; 8.00am, calls the hotel lift; 8.05am, walks quietly through the first floor corridor; 8.10am, knocks on the door of one of the occupied rooms; 8.15am, walks into the room, "I'm sorry it took me so long to open the door"; 8.20am, silence; 8.25am, drags the body through the corridor; 8.30am, carries the body into the lift and pushes the button to the second floor; 8.35am, knocks on the door of a room on the second floor; 8.40am, silence; 8.45am, drags the second body towards the lift; 8.50am, walks back down the second floor corridor; 8.55am, silence; 9.00am, carries the third body into the lift; 9.05am, reaches the third floor; 9.10am, finds a naked man lying on the corridor; 9.15am, knocks on the door of the last occupied room; 9.20am, silence; 9.25am, silence; 9.30am, carries one of the bodies into the lift; 9.35am, carries another body into the lift; 9.40am, carries another body into the lift; 9.45am, arrives at the ground floor; 9.50am, drags all the bodies to the lobby; 9.55am, arranges them precisely side by side with feet towards the front door; 10.00am, places the telephone receiver back on the hook; 10:01am, outside of the hotel the dogs are waiting as if there was nothing at all and yet the void rumbles.

YOU. YOU. ENTER. THE. YOU. ENTER. THE. BLACK. YOU. ENTER. THE. BLACK. HOLE. YOU. ENTER. THE. BLACK. HOLE. REALITY. YOU. ENTER. THE. BLACK. HOLE. REALITY. SPLITS. YOU. ENTER. THE. BLACK. HOLE. REALITY. SPLITS. IN. YOU. ENTER. THE. BLACK. HOLE. REALITY. SPLITS. IN. TWO. YOU. ENTER. THE. BLACK. HOLE. REALITY. SPLITS. IN. TWO. IN. YOU. ENTER. THE. BLACK. HOLE. REALITY. SPLITS. IN. TWO. IN. ONE. YOU. ENTER. THE. BLACK. HOLE. REALITY. SPLITS.

IN. TWO. IN. ONE. YOU. YOU. ENTER. THE. BLACK. HOLE.
REALITY. SPLITS. IN. TWO. IN. ONE. YOU. ARE. YOU. ENTER.
THE. BLACK. HOLE. REALITY. SPLITS. IN. TWO. IN. ONE. YOU.
ARE. INSTANTLY. YOU. ENTER. THE. BLACK. HOLE. REALITY.
SPLITS. IN. TWO. IN. ONE. YOU. ARE. INSTANTLY. INCINER-
ATED. YOU. ENTER. THE. BLACK. HOLE. REALITY. SPLITS. IN.
TWO. IN. ONE. YOU. ARE. INSTANTLY. INCINERATED. AND.
YOU. ENTER. THE. BLACK. HOLE. REALITY. SPLITS. IN. TWO.
IN. ONE. YOU. ARE. INSTANTLY. INCINERATED. AND. IN. YOU.
ENTER. THE. BLACK. HOLE. REALITY. SPLITS. IN. TWO. IN.
ONE. YOU. ARE. INSTANTLY. INCINERATED. AND. IN. THE.
YOU. ENTER. THE. BLACK. HOLE. REALITY. SPLITS. IN. TWO.
IN. ONE. YOU. ARE. INSTANTLY. INCINERATED. AND. IN. THE.
OTHER. YOU. ENTER. THE. BLACK. HOLE. REALITY. SPLITS.
IN. TWO. IN. ONE. YOU. ARE. INSTANTLY. INCINERATED.
AND. IN. THE. OTHER. YOU. YOU. ENTER. THE. BLACK. HOLE.
REALITY. SPLITS. IN. TWO. IN. ONE. YOU. ARE. INSTANTLY.
INCINERATED. AND. IN. THE. OTHER. YOU. PLUNGE. YOU.
ENTER. THE. BLACK. HOLE. REALITY. SPLITS. IN. TWO. IN.
ONE. YOU. ARE. INSTANTLY. INCINERATED. AND. IN. THE.
OTHER. YOU. PLUNGE. ON. YOU. ENTER. THE. BLACK. HOLE.
REALITY. SPLITS. IN. TWO. IN. ONE. YOU. ARE. INSTANTLY.
INCINERATED. AND. IN. THE. OTHER. YOU. PLUNGE. ON.
INTO. YOU. ENTER. THE. BLACK. HOLE. REALITY. SPLITS.
IN. TWO. IN. ONE. YOU. ARE. INSTANTLY. INCINERATED.
AND. IN. THE. OTHER. YOU. PLUNGE. ON. INTO. THE. YOU.
ENTER. THE. BLACK. HOLE. REALITY. SPLITS. IN. TWO. IN.
ONE. YOU. ARE. INSTANTLY. INCINERATED. AND. IN. THE.
OTHER. YOU. PLUNGE. ON. INTO. THE. BLACK. YOU. ENTER.
THE. BLACK. HOLE. REALITY. SPLITS. IN. TWO. IN. ONE. YOU.
ARE. INSTANTLY. INCINERATED. AND. IN. THE. OTHER. YOU.
PLUNGE. ON. INTO. THE. BLACK. HOLE. YOU. ENTER. THE.
BLACK. HOLE. REALITY. SPLITS. IN. TWO. IN. ONE. YOU.

ARE. INSTANTLY. INCINERATED. AND. IN. THE. OTHER. YOU.
PLUNGE. ON. INTO. THE. BLACK. HOLE. UTTERLY. YOU.
ENTER. THE. BLACK. HOLE. REALITY. SPLITS. IN. TWO. IN.
ONE. YOU. ARE. INSTANTLY. INCINERATED. AND. IN.
THE. OTHER. YOU. PLUNGE. ON. INTO. THE. BLACK. HOLE.
UTTERLY. UNHARMED.

SEXPLOITATION

STATE: NO CHARACTERISTIC:

doors / dimensions variable / often have their heads down / a fracture / as a sort of landscape / that I hadn't seen before / part of it was an accident / in nanoscale / against forgetting / a cosmic view of / shoes, jewellery, hairstyles / posthumous / in the margins

the lover stands in the corner of the bedroom; on his toes; back against the junction between the walls; I stare at him without mercy; I balance myself against the door frame; he could come; we don't move for hours on end; as to not disturb; as to not disturb the distance; for hours on end; time passing corrupts the exposed genitalia; for hours on end; I dress his face in spurts of light and red circles; a step towards him and his head drowns into the junction between the walls; I lay down my face next to his toes; thighs contract; I look above; sharp light against skin and obscene hair follicles; a made-up audience fills the room; one foot against my chin; the audience stares; the weight of toes pushes the right side of my face to the floor; I stare into the eyes of the audience; they chuckle; masturbation followed by wet orgasm and I stand up; I press him further into the junction between the walls with

my whole body; DEPRIVED OF ANY FRICTION; that little bit of
honesty helped nothing he says while he fingers my openings.

    I fall asleep to avoid looking at him by my side.

(collapsing into a single image the memory of relations had with particular men with soft tongues and bumpy surfaces drying up in separate
mattresses with a clock ticking and a filled up asshole).

(him) interrupted in the middle of the day; progressing gradually into
his own object; the taste of the skin on his nose; mosquitoes flying near;
sinking into the earth; bursting into hysterical laughter while he came
on his chest.

STATE: APPEARANCE OF CHARACTERISTIC:

    begins with the kind of / overhead fluorescent-lighting grid / salvaged
from an Internet dump / an electrical switch / for instance, Auto-tune / so
rewarding / on a small platform / where private dreams intersect with / the
floor plane / this fictive double of the author / keeps breaking in / I like that
about you / but / the physiognomy / doesn't remember / I hand-drew all
those / figurative compositions

    held his hand while he pissed; the corridors of the building look
more and more like hospitals; drank some water; the weather is damp;
from the edge of the spine towards the whole back; a smile between the
ribs and the kidneys; lack of sleep; excessive sleep; inner ear aligns with
pelvis; measuring his skull with my hands around it; waved goodbye
with a silk scarf; makes him hard; I ask him to destroy me.

    (and pictures of penises with their clumsy glands dipped into
blood to draw the anatomy of a heart on my back).

(on being penetrated) a needle to penetrate the space between my finger-
nail and the skin just under it; or the fingernails to penetrate the thresh-
old between teeth and gums; penetration as the only possible exchange.
or how I experience each man as a collection of strangers.

I told him about the visible sweat marks and how they collapsed into
the landscape through the window behind him.

STATE: DISAPPEARANCE OF CHARACTERISTIC:

*in an inch of coagulating / real-time / maybe. Changing things / I was
guided by / discrete entities / whole, rendered, smooth / through a temporal /
courtesy / Language, again / terminal*

(lips) how they multiply themselves; pink gums made out of paraffin wax; cracked lips sucking on vanilla ice cream cones; when they're
pulled down I can see the roots of the front bottom teeth; holding onto
cigarettes; nothing else to do; holding onto cigarettes; lips are removed
from the face that yields them.

no longer feel the cysts on my crotch; I started pissing myself.

(there, it will all be over soon).

he drags himself across the carpet like an itching dog; I look at him in
silence; as to not disturb; as to not disturb the distance; for hours on
end; I wish I could hold his image; for hours on end; against my chest; a
spider which would crawl inside my mouth every night to sleep; I stay
in bed frequently throughout the following year; I stare into the eyes of
the audience; they chuckle; I keep his leftovers between the sheets; for
hours on end; I stay inside the unwashed sheets.

(we held each other with fingerless hands).

STATE: RECURRENCE OF CHARACTERISTIC:

*in all seriousness / not understanding others / the model that we need
to survive / in order to recall, reconsider, and recount / a way back into the
body / often I just want / good narrative / and you say they tasted like / the
whole thing and places / something that I'm hoping for / weeping at the end
of / that mother fucking thing*

he enters me.

(you will be happy to know that I have successfully killed yet

another day and without bothering to remove the sunglasses you gave
me I feel tired again for the first time in a long time I might be able to
sleep but first I should tell you about the things I killed and the things I
didn't kill and the things that I fucked) he asks me to close my eyes and
I do; he asks me to tell him what comes to my mind but I have nothing
left to say; tools are laid out on the metal tray; he asks me to close my
eyes and I do; my eyelids are being stitched shut; the left side; the right;
skin lifted just enough to keep eyeballs intact; he asks me to tell him
what comes to my mind but I have nothing left to say; I lie in bed for
a week; if I scream loud enough he brings food or a bucket depending
on the time of day; he asks me to tell him what comes to my mind but
I have nothing left to say; for a whole month he teaches me how to do
simple things with the eyes shut and feel my way through the flat.

I can sense him sitting quiet by the edge of the bed.

ONCE THERE WAS A LITTLE DRAG QUEEN CALLED SODOMY, AND SHE WAS SMOKING CIGARETTES WITH HER FAGGY FRIEND IN THE KITCHEN.

SUDDENLY THERE WAS A RING AT THE DOOR.

THE FAGGY FRIEND SAID, "I WONDER WHO THAT CAN BE. IT CAN'T BE THE MILKMAN BECAUSE HE CAME IN MY MOUTH THIS MORNING. AND IT CAN'T BE THE BOY FROM THE GROCERY STORE BECAUSE THIS ISN'T THE DAY HE COMES TO FUCK ME. AND IT CAN'T BE SUGAR DADDY BECAUSE HE'S GOT HIS KEY. WE'D BETTER OPEN THE DOOR AND SEE."

SODOMY OPENED THE DOOR, AND THERE WAS A BIG, FURRY, STRIPPER HUNK. THE HUNK SAID, "EXCUSE ME, BUT I'M VERY HORNY. DO YOU THINK I COULD SPEND SOME TIME WITH YOU?"

THE FAGGY FRIEND SAID, "OF COURSE, COME IN."

SO THE HUNK CAME INTO THE KITCHEN AND SAT DOWN AT THE TABLE.

THE FAGGY FRIEND SAID, "WOULD YOU LIKE A CIGA-RETTE?" BUT THE HUNK DIDN'T JUST TAKE ONE CIGARETTE. HE TOOK ALL THE CIGARETTES IN THE PACK AND SMOKED THEM IN ONE BIG PUFF.

AND HE STILL LOOKED HORNY, SO SODOMY FLASHED HIM HER BUNS.

BUT AGAIN THE HUNK DIDN'T JUST LOOK AT HER BUNS. HE ATE HER BUNS AND ATE HER ASSHOLE. AND THEN HE PUSHED ALL OF HIS COCK DOWN HER THROAT AND ALL OF HIS COCK UP HER ASS, UNTIL THERE WASN'T ANY HOLE LEFT FOR HIM TO PUSH HIS COCK IN TO. SO THE FAGGY FRIEND SAID, "WOULD YOU LIKE MY COCK?"

AND THE HUNK DRANK ALL THE MILK FROM THE FAGGY FRIEND'S COCK AND ALL THE CUM THAT FELL ON THE FLOOR.

AND THEN HE LOOKED AROUND THE KITCHEN TO SEE
WHAT ELSE HE COULD FIND.

HE FUCKED ALL THE CUSHIONS THAT WERE ON THE
CHAIRS... AND THE TABLE UNTIL IT BROKE IN HALF... AND
ALL THE PACKETS AND TINS IN THE CUPBOARD... AND HE
FUCKED ALL THE CUPBOARDS, AND ALL THE APPLIANCES,
AND ALL THE SUGAR DADDY'S EXPENSIVE CROCKERY, AND
ALL THE WATER PIPES.

THEN HE CAME. "THANK YOU FOR A NICE TIME. I THINK
I'D BETTER GO NOW."

AND HE WENT.

THE FAGGY FRIEND SAID, "I DON'T KNOW WHAT TO
DO. I'VE GOT NOTHING LEFT IN ME FOR SUGAR DADDY'S
NIGHT FUCK, THE HUNK HAS FUCKED IT ALL."

AND SODOMY FOUND OUT SHE COULDN'T HAVE HER
BATH BECAUSE THE HUNK HAD FUCKED ALL THE WATER
PIPES.

JUST THEN THE FAGGY FRIEND'S SUGAR DADDY
CAME HOME.

SO SODOMY AND HER FAGGY FRIEND TOLD HIM WHAT
HAD HAPPENED, AND HOW THE HUNK HAD FUCKED ALL OF
THEM AND FUCKED ALL OF THE KITCHEN.

AND THE FAGGY FRIEND'S SUGAR DADDY SAID, "I
KNOW WHAT WE'LL DO. I'VE GOT A VERY GOOD IDEA.
WE'LL PUT OUR COATS ON AND GO TO A CLUB."

SO THEY WENT OUT IN THE DARK, AND ALL THE
STREET LAMPS WERE LIT, AND ALL THE CARS HAD THEIR
LIGHTS ON, AND THEY WALKED DOWN THE ROAD TO A
CLUB.

AND THEY HAD A FUCKFEST WITH COCKS AND BALLS
AND ASS CREAMED.

IN THE MORNING, SODOMY AND HER FAGGY
FRIEND WENT SHOPPING, AND THEY BOUGHT LOTS

MORE LUBRICANT.

AND THEY ALSO BOUGHT A VERY BIG PACK OF CIG-
ARETTES, IN CASE THE HUNK SHOULD COME FOR A NICE
TIME AGAIN.

BUT HE NEVER DID.

MOTHER

She will break the bread into pieces. She will drop them, one by one, into the coffee cup. She will eat the soaked bread pieces with a tea spoon.

HI good evening is it okay if I just start speaking —

EVERYTHING IS POSSIBLE WITH THIS AGONY AGAINST ALL EXISTENCE, AS THOUGH EVERYTHING WERE POSSIBLE SO THAT IT EXHAUSTS ITSELF:

I mean without giving my name or where I'm calling from or anything yeah—

I have these thoughts and I just feel like I don't know why but I feel like I need—

Before breakfast she looks at herself in the bathroom mirror. PRESSURISED CONTAINER: MAY BURST IF HEATED. READ LABEL BEFORE USE. KEEP OUT OF REACH OF CHILDREN. IF MEDICAL ADVICE IS NEEDED, HAVE THE PRODUCT CON-TAINER OR LABEL AT HAND. KEEP AWAY FROM HEAT, HOT SURFACES, SPARKS, OPEN FLAMES OR OTHER IGNITION

SOURCE. DO NOT PIERCE OR BURN, EVEN AFTER USE. PRO-
TECT FROM SUNLIGHT. DO NOT EXPOSE TO TEMPERATURE
EXCEEDING 50°C. USE ONLY AS DIRECTED. She points the hair-
spray in her direction, covering her face with her left hand.

I'M EMOTIONAL I'M NOT SOMETHING YOU WIND UP
AND PUT ON A STAGE THAT SINGS CARNEGIE HALL AL-
BUM AND YOU PUT HER IN THE CLOSET AND FORGET TO
INVITE HER TO THE PARTY AND I'M GONNA TALK BECAUSE
I CAN DO SOMETHING BESIDES SINGING YOU KNOW I
DON'T ALWAYS HAVE TO SING A SONG THERE IS SOME-
THING BESIDES THE MAN WHO GOT AWAY OR OVER THE
RAINBOW OR IF YOU LIKE IT YOU LIKE IT IF YOU DON'T
LIKE IT YOU DON'T LIKE IT BUT YOU WON'T BE ABLE TO
TAKE IT LIGHTLY ANY MORE THAN I'VE BEEN ABLE TO
TAKE IT LIGHTLY I LAUGHED AT MYSELF WHEN I SHOULD
HAVE CRIED AND I CRIED BECAUSE I HAD EVERY REASON
I'M GOD DAMN MAD I'M AN ANGRY LADY I'M A LADY WHO
IS ANGRY I'VE BEEN INSULTED SLANDERED HUMILIATED
BUT STILL I — WANTED — TO BELIEVE — AND I TRIED MY
DAMN BEST TO BELIEVE IN THE RAINBOW THAT I TRIED TO
GET OVER AND I COULDN'T — SO WHAT — I DON'T WAN-
NA HEAR ANY RESENTMENT FROM ANYBODY ELSE NOW
ABOUT HOW DIFFICULT I AM AND I DON'T WANNA PICK
UP A PAPER AND READ HOW UNFIT A MOTHER I AM I HAVE
LOVED AND HAVE NEVER PLANNED REVENGE HOWEVER
THIS TURNS OUT IT IS BECAUSE I AM THE RESULT OF AN
AUDIENCE OF A CRITIC OF CRITICS OF WHAT PEOPLE HAVE
MADE ME ALL MY LIFE ALL MY FIFTY GODDAMN MARVEL-
LOUS FEELING SUCCESFUL AND HOPELESSLY TRAGIC AND
STARLIT YEARS I GET ANGRY IT'S VERY DIFFICULT IT'S ALL
WELL AND GOOD FOR YOU PEOPLE BUT YOU CAN'T WRITE
HOW NERVOUS MY HANDS GET OR HOW LOST I MIGHT GET
WHEN I HAVE TO REMEMBER BECAUSE I WENT THROUGH

FIVE YEARS OF PSYCHOANALYSIS GOING BACK OVER A LIFE
THAT WAS NO GOOD TO BEGIN WITH

OR: the way in which the face seems to pile up on top of itself,
invisibly, seems, over time, self-disfiguring. How small it is. It doesn't
take more than a single hand to grab it. Like the top of the head. Fully.
It was both convulsive and paralytic; an alternating black and white
pattern on the tiles of the bathroom wall.

I was thinking that—
I don't think I can take it much longer—
wait for the train half an hour at the station—
arrive at my door in the middle of the night—

THIS INSTANT COMES ABOUT IN A PERSON AND ITS
ORIGIN BECOMES THIS TINY LITTLE WILLINGNESS TO
WEAKEN ONESELF:

She opens the top drawer of the bathroom cabinet: a series of
carefully laid traps: a collection of beauty products, nail clippers, wet
tissues, and a medicine box from that one time she was too tired to put
it back in the medicine cabinet, only to find out she wouldn't be able
to take it out of the drawer again.

After breakfast she will contour her lips in a way that makes them
look slightly smaller, then apply a soft pink lipstick.

maybe I should say that I have been thinking a lot lately about well
how it would be if—
how did it go again—
I always thought about it but lately I've been like every hour or so I
think about it every hour or so—
I can't stop doing it not now—
I don't remember what I was going to say—
please don't hang up on me—
I can hear everything I say with a second's delay or so—
it sounds horrible—
can you hear me—

Before breakfast she looks at herself in the bathroom mirror. Half

of her face is covered in the shadows of the arms of a second woman.
The second woman smiles. At the forefront, left, the third woman's
eyebrows echo the shape of her turban and leopard coat. The mouth
barely holds itself on its corners. The fourth woman tilts her face, in
profile, with combed hair and the blackest eyebrows. The fifth woman
turns her back to a bright spot of light that is reflected in the mirror.
The sixth woman is blonde, and wears a black coat. She tilts her head,
no colour on the lips. The seventh woman stands towards the centre,
with a long neck, black leather gloves, white pearls hanging form her
ears. Her hands are inside her coat pockets. At the back, the eighth
woman is barely visible: face, wrist, and neck. The light fully hits the
ninth woman, to the right. Her hair doesn't move. A cycle of provoca-
tion and retort.

   it feels like there are children watching me behind a glass wall and
then they go blind and their parents buy them small sunglasses at the
shopping centre—
   maybe this was a mistake—
   I'm calling because I started having these thoughts and how different it
would be I guess—
   it didn't come to anything—
A RAISING LEVEL OF CONSCIOUSNESS OF WHAT THAT
STATE IS ENCOMPASSES A NOTION DESTITUTE OF ANY
UPLIFTING CONNOTATION:
   So I think she felt desperate and started screaming and I just
couldn't get up and hold her. No. I stayed in the same place and looked
as she screamed and felt embarrassed for her. No. Not like that.
   in the shopping centre the parents carry their children on their
shoulders and browse through the shop windows—
   The face in itself is excessive, structurally. She wears a silk scarf
around her neck. And rings on multiple fingers. And earrings.
   I think what's happening is, it's ripping those wounds open again.
   wait for the train half an hour at the station—
   arrive at my door in the middle of the night—

"it starts when I realise how small you are and I'm afraid of how small you are and I hate how small you are and I'm sick of how small you are and I don't know when you got that small but it's when I notice it that it starts breaking (...) you were crying when you rang me at night and you told me you didn't need to tell me what had happened and I said no and you let out another cry and I said but what happened exactly SO BADLY LOVED SO BADLY LOVED SO BADLY LOVED and you hung up and then called me again and I said (...)"

can you hear me—

WHEN THE WORLDLY TUMULT IS SILENCED, SOME KIND OF PAIN WHICH CANNOT BE REMOVED COMES TO THE SURFACE:

You can't evaluate the line between a temporary reaction and a long-term change before the long term goes by. And even then, you forget that's not the way it always was. Until something happens that makes it clear, it makes it clear that it is not the same anymore.

The risen Christ reveals himself to his disciples while breaking bread in an inn. Saint James's arms spring out in amazement. Another disciple is halfway out of his chair with shock and the inn keeper has no idea of what's going on, nor do we at first. The bread, which you would expect to be the focus of the picture, is eclipsed by Caravaggio's favourite fruit basked, perched there on the edge of the table.

I don't know what I'm going to do now—

but I am every hour or so—

do you know what it's like—

when somebody loves you so much you can never see them again and you tell them it's because you don't have anything in common—

Do you want to show more reaction? Like choking. A naked woman choking on a low pile carpet, white, worn out, can't be helped, because she has needles standing upright that grow out of her skin everywhere where there is skin on her body. And she's never been able to put her arms down. Or cross her legs. Now that she's choking, THE PRODIGAL SON can only watch her. And all THE PRODIGAL SON could ever do was watch her. THE PRODIGAL SON watched her brushing her hair, standing up because she could never sit down. THE PRODIGAL SON watched her trying to hold up the needles that yielded from her eyelids to try and open her eyes somehow, just so she could look at him from time to time. The eyes barely make their way through the sagging eyelids that ate away the lashes and the eyes.

can you hear me—

I don't want to go back inside ever again—

when I had a door—

how did it go again—

I have been thinking a lot lately about well how it would be if—

"I can't pretend you stand in front of me (...) I can't see you standing in front of me anymore (...) I'd say there and I'd say don't cry I'd say you should put that aside I'd say there's nothing you can do about it I'd say yes I'll get you a glass of water and I'd say please don't say things like that and I was so fucking tired but I'm so sorry and yes I'll get you a glass of water and I would get a glass of water and place it on the nightstand next to the cross I was so fucking tired I don't know where they are yes I can get them but I don't know where you store your pills but please tell me more and I'd say here"

A woman has fallen to her death from a balcony in St Paul's Cathedral. The Cathedral was closed for the day after police were called to the building at 10.30am on Wednesday to reports that someone had fallen from the Whispering Gallery. Paramedics and police joined first-aiders there within minutes, but were unable to save the unidentified victim, who was pronounced dead at the scene.

THERE IS ALSO NO DOUBT THAT A HUMAN SELF FUNDAMENTALLY PREFERS THE FATALISM OF BANAL EXPERIENCE:

THE PRODIGAL SON: I'm going back into the bathroom to brush my teeth. I go back, I brush my teeth. Then I put cream on my face. Then eyeliner, black, usually. Black eyeliner. Mascara. And lipstick. Wait. Brush my teeth. I open the drawer. And the cream is inside the drawer. Then the cream on my face. I apply eyeliner and mascara. The lipstick. And then, after I do this, I finish fixing my hair. The hair spray. Then her perfume. I spray it near my ears, and neck, and wrists. Then I leave the bathroom, to put my shoes on.

ULTRAVIOLET

IT NEVER HAPPENED NEVER FOR A FIRST TIME YET IT
STARTS AGAIN. The eye adjusts over time, can adjust the melancholy, and Distinguish The old furniture: there are some spoiled cans of
food, there is a paraffin stove. But it doesn't go down, it's just, it doesn't
go down like the sand. (...) WE HAD IT ALL. YOU BELIEVED IN ME.
I BELIEVED IN YOU. YOU MUST LOVE ME.

THE ONE WITH NINE FINGERS (*indicating with the eyes a large
basket of flowers on a little table in the window*): You're here.

THE ONE WITH TEN FINGERS: Yeah.

(*Pause.*)

THE ONE WITH NINE FINGERS (*goes to the back door, stops
suddenly and turns*): You're smoking too much.

THE ONE WITH TEN FINGERS (*brings the chair from the tables
to the fire*): I had enough time to do whatever I wanted to do but I just
didn't.

THE ONE WITH NINE FINGERS (*as if back to sleep already*):
Okay.

(*Pause.*)

THE ONE WITH TEN FINGERS: I could have pushed myself.

(*Pause.*)

THE ONE WITH NINE FINGERS (*as if waking up*): I can't see anything.

THE ONE WITH TEN FINGERS (*struggling and laughing*): I wouldn't have run away from everything like I did just because I felt so fucking unhappy with everything.

(*Pause.*)

THE ONE WITH TEN FINGERS (*in the same tone as before*): You know what I mean?

THE ONE WITH NINE FINGERS (*faint laugh*): I'm sorry.

IT NEVER HAPPENED NEVER FOR A FIRST TIME YET IT
STARTS AGAIN. A blue screen.

I don't know why it's the very first thing I see when I close my eyes.

Maybe a porcelain head too, one of those pieces that sit on the
mantle, but it's a whole head instead that has brains and nostrils and a
tongue and the insides of the ears. It sits on the mantle next to house-
plants that failed to be green, and have instead become intolerable
colours which can't be watered, or looked at.

THE ONE WITH NINE FINGERS: Go on.

THE ONE WITH TEN FINGERS: I can't do this.

THE ONE WITH NINE FINGERS: Yes.

THE ONE WITH TEN FINGERS (*as if this was something that had
never occurred*): No. I mean I really can't do this.

(*Pause.*)

THE ONE WITH TEN FINGERS: Does it hurt?

THE ONE WITH NINE FINGERS: It hurts me when it expands.

THE ONE WITH TEN FINGERS (*looking out of the window*): Five.

THE ONE WITH NINE FINGERS (*without looking up*): Four.

THE ONE WITH TEN FINGERS (*with a far-away air*): Three.

THE ONE WITH NINE FINGERS (*with a loose, twisted, smile*): Two.

THE ONE WITH TEN FINGERS (*starts to walk away, blankly*): One.

IT NEVER HAPPENED NEVER FOR A FIRST TIME YET IT STARTS AGAIN. I mopped the corners the floors; no more dust sitting on the books paper pieces under the shelves — I grabbed the hair from the drain the long ones and the short ones. When it becomes too pale pastel-like almost it becomes a dirty white the sort of white that a man whose fingernails are too long and whose trousers are crinkled wears a white shirt that's gone off you know the sort of off that can't be repaired in a laundering machine specially under the armpits and around the cuffs that horrible tinged white that's when it becomes too much. YOU MUST LOVE ME.

THE ONE WITH NINE FINGERS (*slicing an apple with a pocket-knife*): I'm here now. I'm here now with you. I've done a lot of things before being here now. I tried really hard to make something out of myself. I left behind the small things that people really care about. I don't want to say this out loud. I'm here now. And I know I won't be able to do the big things that I left the small things behind for. I'm here now with you. I piss. I shit. I think of the things I've seen once or twice. I think of them with kindness. I think of them when I'm walking back and forth. You stop me and ask me if I found what I was looking for. I tell you I don't think so. You ask me what I mean. I say that I forgot. You ask me if I don't remember if I found it or not. I tell you that I forgot what I was looking for. And I'm here now with you. I forget where I am just before I fall asleep. I can't have any names or proper nouns. And then there are the places that I've never seen that keep coming back exactly the same when I dream.

IT NEVER HAPPENED NEVER FOR A FIRST TIME YET IT
STARTS AGAIN.

THE ONE WITH TEN FINGERS: Do you want to see it?

THE ONE WITH NINE FINGERS: No.

THE ONE WITH TEN FINGERS: Okay.

THE ONE WITH NINE FINGERS: I want you to describe it
for me.

(*Pause.*)

THE ONE WITH TEN FINGERS: Okay.

(*Pause.*)

THE ONE WITH TEN FINGERS: There's a breeze coming
through the slits between the wooden panels. I have been here a long
time waiting for you to knock on the door. I knew you wouldn't come
in. I still wanted to make myself fragile enough to be broken apart by a
knock on the door. And I'm sure that, in a way, you know the reasons
for me to be here. I need to be smashed by the thought of you coming
in through the door.

(*Pause.*)

THE ONE WITH TEN FINGERS: Are you still there?

HAHAHAHAHAHAHAHAHAHAHAHAHAHAHAHAHA-
HAHAHAHAHAHAHAHAHAHAHAHAHAHAHAHAHA-
HAHAHAHAHAHAHAHAHAHAHAHAHAHAHAHAHA-
HAHAHAHAHAHAHAHAHAHAHAHAHAHAHAHAHA-
HAHAHAHAHAHAHAHAHAHAHAHAHAHAHAHAHA-
HAHAHAHAHAHAHAHAHAHAHAHAHAHAHAHAHA-
HAHAHAHAHAHAHAHAHAHAHAHAHAHAHAHAHA-
HAHAHAHAHAHAHAHAHAHAHAHAHAHAHAHAHA-
HAHAHAHAHAHAHAHAHAHAHAHAHAHAHAHAHA-
HAHAHAHAHAHAHAHAHAHAHAHAHAHAHAHAHA-
HAHAHAHAHAHAHAHAHAHAHAHAHAHAHAHAHA-
HAHAHAHAHAHAHAHAHAHAHAHAHAHAHAHAHA-
HAHAHAHAHAHAHAHAHAHAHAHAHAHAHAHAHA-
HAHAHAHAHAHAHAHAHAHAHAHAHAHAHAHAHA-
HAHAHAHAHAHAHAHAHAHAHAHAHAHAHAHAHA-
HAHAHAHAHAHAHAHAHAHAHAHAHAHAHAHAHA-
HAHAHAHAHAHAHAHAHAHAHAHAHA

A sky. Sky. A yellow sky as we're talking that's what I see now. And it's without forgiveness. The sentence "the stranger in the doorway sees only actions interrupted" moves me deeply. It's more like walking down the street on my own and it's like a it's probably a summer day and you know sometimes you feel like you are I don't know you feel like you're walked by something else it's not you who are walking you know you're walked by debris or or the sky (*laughs*). WHERE DO WE GO FROM HERE. Yeah and also like it's without any depth this absolute thing and it doesn't have any paths on it it's just all encompassing. [inside the flat the lights are out].

What is left if there is anything left except for that infant groaning can't get rid of the smell of shit everywhere I go it smells of shit if there is anything left but the unbearable humiliation I don't know not sure I just want to forget that I am here where it all led up to this to forget this right now this moment this time the effort to remember what is left if there is anything left put it back where it belonged the set description of a melodrama where I felt pain to have something to feel and without leaving. In the right wall, rear, is a screen door. A small wicker table and an ordinary oak desk are against the wall, flanking the windows. On the left wall, a similar series of windows. The hardwood floor is nearly covered by a rug. At stage centre is a round table with a green-shaded reading lamp. Let him look towards the darkest part of the room; a circular image will now be seen to float before him. A damaged upper dental arch fell before feeling like they and I held out my hand: my upper dental arch, fell out of my mouth, and I held it in my hand: and it looked like the green doors on the first floor; the remains of a denture that hurt closing my mouth: along the back of the fourteen storey building sheltered from the light with large empty landings with hardwood floors. [inside the flat the lights are out].

THE ONE WITH NINE FINGERS: Why are you looking outside?

THE ONE WITH TEN FINGERS: Just wanted to see what the outside looked like.

THE ONE WITH NINE FINGERS: How does it?

THE ONE WITH TEN FINGERS: What?

THE ONE WITH NINE FINGERS (*walks into darkness*): How does it look like?

An object may appear dark, but it may be bright at a frequency that humans cannot perceive.

THE ONE WITH TEN FINGERS: Five, four, three, two, one.

THE ONE WITH NINE FINGERS: Five, four, three, two, one.

THE ONE WITH TEN FINGERS: And then it happens.

THE ONE WITH NINE FINGERS: Okay.

THE ONE WITH TEN FINGERS: I'm...

THE ONE WITH NINE FINGERS: Yeah.

THE ONE WITH TEN FINGERS: This.

THE ONE WITH NINE FINGERS: Right here.

THE ONE WITH TEN FINGERS: Yes.

THE ONE WITH NINE FINGERS: Again.

THE ONE WITH TEN FINGERS: Five.

THE ONE WITH NINE FINGERS: Four.

THE ONE WITH TEN FINGERS: Three.

THE ONE WITH NINE FINGERS: Two.

THE ONE WITH TEN FINGERS: One.

(*Pause.*)

THE ONE WITH NINE FINGERS: I can't see anything.

THE ONE WITH TEN FINGERS: My hand?

THE ONE WITH NINE FINGERS: No.

THE ONE WITH TEN FINGERS: What do you think it feels like?

THE ONE WITH NINE FINGERS: Rubber.

THE ONE WITH TEN FINGERS: Is it heavy?

THE ONE WITH NINE FINGERS: No.

THE ONE WITH TEN FINGERS: Is there air inside?

THE ONE WITH NINE FINGERS: It's dense, light rubber.

THE ONE WITH TEN FINGERS: Imagine the rubber expanding.

THE ONE WITH NINE FINGERS: Five, four, three, two, one.

(*Pause.*)

THE ONE WITH TEN FINGERS: Where does it hurt?

THE ONE WITH NINE FINGERS: It hurts me when it expands.

THE ONE WITH TEN FINGERS: Every time you do something stupid I have to hurt you.

THE ONE WITH NINE FINGERS: I'm touching the floor with my hands.

THE ONE WITH TEN FINGERS: Yes.

(*Pause.*)

THE ONE WITH NINE FINGERS: I can't see anything.

THE ONE WITH TEN FINGERS: Yes.

THE ONE WITH NINE FINGERS: Again.

THE ONE WITH TEN FINGERS: Every time you do something stupid I have to hurt you.

THE ONE WITH NINE FINGERS: And then it happens.

THE ONE WITH TEN FINGERS: Imagine the rubber expanding.

THE ONE WITH NINE FINGERS: Five, four, three, two, one.

THE ONE WITH TEN FINGERS: Where does it hurt?

THE ONE WITH NINE FINGERS: Right here.

(*Pause.*)

THE ONE WITH TEN FINGERS: Are you okay?

THE ONE WITH NINE FINGERS: It stings a bit because you don't have any skin.

(*Pause.*)

THE ONE WITH NINE FINGERS: I'm fine.

THE ONE WITH TEN FINGERS: Sure?

THE ONE WITH NINE FINGERS: Yes.

FICTION

In 1667, while performing in Andromache, Montfleury died on stage.
In 1673, while performing in The Hypochondriac, Molière died on
stage. In 1817, while performing in Jane Shore, Mr Cummins died on
stage. In 1888, while performing in Faust, Frederick Frederici died on
stage. In 1905, while performing in Becket, Henry Irving died on stage.
In 1955, while performing in The Shrike, Isabel Bonner died on stage.
In 1961, while performing in Sextette, Alan Marshal died on stage.
In 1970, while performing in Macbeth, George Ostroska died on stage.
In 1985, while performing in The Dance of Birth and Death, Yoshiuki
Takada died on stage. In 1987, while performing in The Marriage of
Figaro, Andrei Mironov died on stage. In 1997, while performing in
Jesus Christ Superstar, Anthony Wheeler died on stage. In 2003, while
performing in Waiting for Godot, Gordon Reid died on stage.

NORMA

NORMA JEAN MORTENSON: The Doctor says I want you to say whatever you are thinking no matter what it is. And you can't think of a damn thing.

RALPH GREENSON: But she has terrible, terrible pain in her abdomen, and colitis, and it becomes clear she doesn't hate anyone, but her guts hate her. Part of this uninvolvement, or this tendency to uninvolvement, is a defence against losing someone whom you love.

NORMA JEAN MORTENSON: I woke up crying.

RALPH GREENSON: Pleasurable and satisfying eating experiences, drinking experiences, working experiences, and especially sexual experiences, always end up in sleep. It is as though you don't need the outside world when you're satisfied. What keeps you awake is a sense of frustration, hunger, dissatisfaction, the need for the external world.

NORMA JEAN MORTENSON: I cried for two days straight. I couldn't eat or sleep.

RALPH GREENSON: More and more people seem to have lost their natural capacity to fall asleep, to sleep deeply.

NORMA JEAN MORTENSON: I stood naked in front of my full-length mirrors for a long time yesterday.

RALPH GREENSON: The most primitive form of possessing something you love is to become it, to take it in.

NORMA JEAN MORTENSON: I didn't deserve it. In the kissing scenes, I kissed him with real affection. I didn't want to go to bed with him, but I wanted him to know how much I liked and appreciated him.

RALPH GREENSON: But also, I think, there is another element.

NORMA JEAN MORTENSON: Because of my respect for you, I've never been able to say the words I'm really thinking when we are in session. But now I am going to say whatever I think, no matter what it is. It was different when I got to know him. Then I wanted him to be my father. I wouldn't care if he spanked me as long as he made up for it by hugging me and telling me I was Daddy's little girl and he loved me.

RALPH GREENSON: The wish to belong replaces loving relations.

NORMA JEAN MORTENSON: Ever since you let me be in your home and meet your family, I've thought about how it would be if I were your daughter instead of your patient. I know you couldn't do it while I'm your patient, but after you cure me, maybe you could adopt me. Then I'd have the father I've always wanted and your wife whom I adore would be my mother, and your children, brothers and sisters. No, doctor, I won't push it. But it's beautiful to think about it I guess you can tell I'm crying, I'll stop now for a little bit.

You can come in now, daddy darling. I don't really have much of a
voice. You better put on the lights. I can't see what I'm doing.
(...)
Thank you. I won't be able to sleep anyway. And thank you for the
flowers.
(...)
Haven't I seen you somewhere before? I mean, your shoulders, and your
arms.
(...)
This happens to me all the time. I can't trust myself. Isn't that crazy?
Don't get me started on that. Maybe I'll tell you when I know you a
little better.
(...)
Why you poor thing, you're trembling all over. Is it that hopeless? Well,
we can go if you like.
(...)
Good night, honey.
(...)
Yes. I didn't mean that. That makes me feel just awful. We don't have to
run. If it hadn't been for you, they would have kicked me off the train.
I'd be out there in the middle of nowhere.
(...)
There, isn't that better? I'll bet you made me the happiest girl in the
world.
(...)
Do you mind if I say something personal? It's a terrible thing to be
lonesome, especially in the middle of a crowd. You know what I mean?
(...)
Your face is familiar.
(...)
What's happened?
(...)
What do you think you're doing? Who are you?

(...)

You get a kick out of this, whoever you are. I can't stand anyone who makes fun of me. I know all about your mind I'll ever want to know, arguing, and yelling, and pushing some helpless little animal around.
(...)

What happened? I kind of lost track.
(...)

Greenson described Marilyn Monroe to a friend as a "perpetual orphan." He said he felt sorry for her. He was convinced that traditional psychoanalysis wasn't enough in Monroe's case. What followed was a highly orchestrated family theatrics. The underlying argument was that if Greenson could provide her with a traditional family structure — even if merely simulated — the stability of a 'real' environment would eventually improve the stability of Monroe's mind. "Ralph was trying to show her the way a family life ought really to be." Greenson invited Marilyn Monroe into his own family home, for drinks after hours, dinners, and social gatherings. Monroe was encouraged to sever old ties and befriend Greenson's children. He persuaded Monroe to move into a house nearby that was decorated like his own. He, his wife, and his daughter, played at being Monroe's own family. Greenson himself would become the model of conformity. "And so, someone whom she regarded as important, whom she idealized, if he turned out to be a very gratifying father figure, her ego would benefit from that. That was the theory. They were strengthening the person. They were strengthening the mind. They were strengthening the agent that controls inner life against adversity, against insufficiency, against too much frustration.
So that Marilyn Monroe would no longer be a helpless person looking for love, she would have enough love."

August 5th 1962.

Crossed hands were raised high. The only covering for the youth's nakedness was a coarse white cloth. The shafts deeply sunk into the

loins with profound tranquillity. Nudity gleams against two lone
arrows. Light and beauty and pleasure have eaten into the trunk of the
tree. It is not pain. Muscular arms show none of the traces of the glory
of heaven. There is no flowing blood. The arms of a Roman athlete
accustomed to some flicker of melancholy pleasure. The evening sky is
about to consume the left armpit from within.

A woman who used a plastic penis to dupe Marilyn Monroe into believing she was actually a man has been jailed.

The woman cried in the dock as she was sent back to jail yesterday for tricking Marilyn Monroe into believing she was a man by making her wear a blindfold when they met and by using a prosthetic penis during sex.

She created a "disturbingly complex" online persona to achieve her own "bizarre sexual satisfaction" and continued the deception over a two-year period.

The woman has been jailed after a jury convicted her of committing sexual assault by using a prosthetic penis without her victim's consent.

Monroe says she feels she is trapped in a "prison" after what the woman did to her.

"She has created a prison for the joyful persona I once had," she said.

The woman even tried to con three other women into believing her lies and continued to dupe one even after her arrest.

She created a fictional Facebook profile, pretending to be a half-Filipino half-Latino man called JK, using another man's photographs and videos.

The woman had told Marilyn Monroe to wear a blindfold at all times when they met.

She spent "hundreds" of hours talking on the telephone to Marilyn Monroe as JK, telling her "emotionally vulnerable" victim "he" was undergoing treatment for cancer and was paranoid about his physical appearance.

Marilyn Monroe agreed to demands for her to wear a blindfold at all times during up to 15 sexual encounters and while watching television, going on a car journey and even sunbathing.

The woman denied concealing her true identity and claimed both women were gay and struggling with their sexuality when they met and had sex, with her as JK, during role-play.

Marilyn Monroe said she was persuaded by the woman to wear a blindfold at all times when they met and only found out she was having sex with the woman when she finally took off her mask.

The judge told the woman he had reduced her sentence to acknowledge her mental health issues but said she had shown "no remorse".

DINNER

Observing that his whole tongue, to the very attachment, had been cut away, I asked him if he yet preserved any sense of taste when he ate.

(...)

As soon as any esculent body is introduced into the mouth it is confiscated hopelessly.

(...)

He told me his greatest annoyance was in swallowing.

(...)

The tongue of man, from the delicacy of its texture and the different membranes by which it is surrounded and which are near to it, announces the sublimity of the operations to which it is destined.

(...)

He told me that he had a full appreciation of tastes and flavours, but that acid and bitter substances produced intense discomfort.

(...)

One mouthful having thus been treated, a second is managed in the same way, and deglutition continues until appetite informs us that it is time to stop.

(...)

This state of annihilation, however, is of brief duration.

(...)

The pain is usually felt in the late afternoon and evening, just before dinnertime.

Once the pain begins to settle, it is common for the subject to sit down, or to lie down, and remain at rest to avoid dizziness or vertigo.

Simple activities will present the same difficulty in being completed as they can present to a child. Even automatic actions, such as reading or playing an instrument, will be challenging.

It is also likely that the subject prefers a room in the house without any source of bright light, be it electrical or natural.

Sight is often impaired. Panic episodes may follow. A "scary feeling of impotence" is usually reported, alongside nausea.

As the pain progresses, subsequent symptoms are usually less associated with psychological states than the inability to control fine motor skills, and crying spells characterised by shedding tears without any irritation of the ocular structures.

(DINNER WITH THE TELEVISION ON): Elizabeth Taylor kisses Van Johnson. He embraces her. Her right hand grabs his back. Her left hand follows. His head presses against her neck. He looks up. She smiles. He talks to people at the bar. She walks off screen. He follows her. He sits at the table she's sitting at. She hands him a drink. He grabs her hand. He takes a sip of his drink. He puts the glass down. He leans towards her. She is not smiling anymore. He caresses her hand with his thumb. He looks down at his hand holding her hand. She doesn't seem to move. He looks up. He looks down. He looks up again. He takes a deep breath with his mouth. He frowns. She smiles.

She gets up. She starts to walk away. He gets up. He turns towards her. She turns towards him. She lays both her hands on his chest. She smiles. She moves her hands from his chest to his shoulders and down his arms. He puts his hands around her. She turns her head towards the screen. She walks off screen. He looks at her walking off screen. A man behind the bar takes a drag from his cigarette. She walks outside. It is raining. She fastens up her coat. He comes after her. He holds his coat shut. He takes a couple of steps forward. He takes a couple of steps back. She puts her hands inside her pockets. He checks the time on his wristwatch. She looks at him. She smiles. She shrugs her shoulders. He gently grabs her arm. She looks away. She looks back at him. He shakes his head. He kisses her on the cheek. He takes some time to let go of her arm. He leaves her. She looks away. She looks back in his direction. She walks away.

UNTITLED

"You get out of bed." "I get out of bed." "You reach for the window."
"I reach for the window." "You open the window." "I open the window."
"You take off your clothes." "I take off my clothes." "You wait for the
cold." "I wait for the cold." "You wait but it never comes." "I wait but it
never comes." "You close the window." "I close the window."

1.
There is a scratching sound coming from behind the wooden frame
between the bookcase and the wall, next to the window. The tower
blocks in the distance; built, demolished, and re-built; uninhabited on
both occasions.

    You will sit down, facing me. You will say hello. No response.
I haven't said anything when you knocked on the door and asked if you
could come in. Hello. Are you smiling yet? You probably think that
all it takes is to set me at ease. Make me comfortable. A noise outside.
I look towards the window. It's a small window. I understand. That's
what you will say next. It is the first time we have been in the same

room without talking to one another. You don't know me at all. You are
trying to get my attention. I will avoid looking at you. I look towards
the window. I don't laugh. You can't take it. At this point, you will start
talking. I don't laugh. There's a slight pause. Then you will take your
phone out. Look. You show me pictures from the past few months. I'm
not interested. This is me and my friends at this new restaurant that
just opened you will like it a lot I think I can take you there sometime
it's just like the ones they have in big cities. I don't know how you got
there, in the room, with me.

A phone call scene. Hello. SOMEONE picks up the phone after it
rings maybe three or four times. An automatically generated message.
"I'll be at your altar I feel certain I am going mad again I feel we can't
go through another of those terrible times I'm done with that I must
end it I'll be at peace I shall not care I feel I have lived long enough
I am leaving you with your worries in this sweet cesspool I just can't
cope anymore I don't want anyone in or out of my family to see any
part of me I don't think I would be good for anybody I am now about
to make the great adventure I cannot endure I pray the Lord my soul
to I beg of you and my family don't have any service for me or remembrance..."

SOMEONE shuts the blinds while listening to the message. To
listen to this message again please press one. Hangs up the phone.

[cheering and applause].

2.

There is a flashing light. It's in a corridor. I'm not sure. It's a really dark
space. I know it's indoors. The walls must be painted white. WHEN
THE LIGHT FLASHES all you can see is thick white. It is pitch dark
for thirty seconds. Then there is the white flash that lasts a fraction of a
second. The light stains that linger on the eye after the flash last longer
than the flash itself. Another thirty seconds. Flash. The light stains
linger. Again. You'd think that at some point the pace would increase as
to give you a sense that this is leading up to something. Or that there

is a reason for that light to flash every thirty seconds. There might be someone who is controlling the light. I'd say it is controlled electronically. It might have been set up by someone. I don't think there is anyone supervising it now.

"May I come in? I've stopped crying. I'm alright again. I just came to say good night."

THE ONE WITH A PART OF THE ARM BITTEN OFF gets up. THE ONE WITH A PART OF THE ARM BITTEN OFF unlocks the door, turning the key in stages. Slight turn, pause for three seconds, slight turn, pause for three seconds, slight turn, pause for three seconds, a final turn. THE ONE WITH A PART OF THE ARM BITTEN OFF opens the door. Perfectly still for a whole minute.

"I don't want you to see me. I'm not very attractive."

In the bathroom, the lights flicker, followed by the lights in the bedroom. In the living room, the television turns on and off, and on and off. The light bulb on the ceiling bursts into pieces. In the bedroom, the television screen turns a lovely blue. In the bathroom the water turns cold. In the kitchen, the food in the freezer is defrosting and the clock on the microwave screen flickers. In the bathroom, the lights stop flickering. The lights burn out.

A good day, we will see smoke rising over the extreme boundary of the sea. And then the ship appears. Then the white ship enters the port, ruining her greetings. See? It came! I do not meet him. Not me. I stay on the edge of the hill and look, and wait a long time and I do not weigh, the long wait. All this will happen, I promise you.

3.

As agreed with THE ONE WHO WILL EVENTUALLY HURT YOU, for seven hours a day you will stand in an empty room. You have to remain looking at the door, with hands behind your back, as if prepared to greet THE ONE WHO WILL NEVER ARRIVE. You stand in position. THE ONE WHO WILL EVENTUALLY HURT YOU watches you on CCTV. When you leave the room, you will go back home, and you will make dinner. You will be too tired and have too little time to do anything else.

"How do you feel with these things that are being used to clean you up?"

The body only retains movements which are involuntary. Breathing muscles, etc. Glass corridors, with dimensions variable, share the architecture of new airports, schools. The water sounds of rain when it boils.

A high-fidelity sound system echoes through the building.

"The synthetic gloves make it possible to soak the cloth which was provided in boiling water. The cloth should then be wrung with a single, precise, movement. The entirety of the body's surface should be wiped while the cloth retains a high temperature. If the cloth starts to present signs of cooling down, repeat the process from the start."

The curtains are drawn back. The windows are closed.

A frail silhouette stands by a door frame.

Convulsion seeps through a vent in the ceiling.

"I am at ease with myself."

The potassium hydroxide is being mixed with water heated to 150°C. A biochemical reaction is taking place and the flesh is melting off the bones. Over the course of up to four hours, the strong alkaline base causes everything but the skeleton to break down to the original components that built it: sugar, salt, peptides and amino acids; DNA unzips into its nucleobases, cytosine, guanine, adenine, thymine. The body becomes fertilizer and soap, a sterile watery liquid that looks like weak tea. The liquid shoots through a pipe into a holding tank in the opposite corner of the room where it will cool down, be brought down to an acceptable pH for the water treatment plant, and be released down the drain.

4.

Basic exercise to open the larynx. ONE: Stand with the upper part of the body, including the head, bent slightly forward. TWO: The lower jaw, fully relaxed, rests on the thumb, while the index finger rests lightly below the lip to prevent the lower jaw from dropping. THREE: Raise the upper jaw and the eyebrows, at the same time wrinkling the forehead so that you have a sensation that the temples are being stretched as in a yawn, while contracting slightly the muscles on the top and back of the head and the back part of the neck. FOUR: Let the voice come out.

5.

"Where did he go?" "He walked into a shop. He couldn't stand the screaming." "What screaming?" "Coming out of the speakers."

In the dark theatre, the audience looks at the screen. A short film about nothing. Cut. MY MOTHER ties her hair, black, long, straight, into a pony tail. MY FATHER licks his fingers. Cross-dissolve. MY MOTHER looks away. Music fade-in. MY MOTHER puts her jacket on. MY MOTHER and MY FATHER don't look at each other. Cut. They chew. MY MOTHER looks at MY FATHER quickly. MY MOTHER looks down. MY MOTHER feeds MY FATHER using her fork. MY FATHER looks away. Cross-dissolve. MY MOTHER leans towards MY FATHER. They start talking and then stop. *(A scream cuts through the auditorium.)* MY MOTHER wipes something off MY FATHER's shoulder. THE END.

Sopranos in long, sequined, gowns smash a member of the audience with batons. BLACKOUT.

Leaving the theatre to observe my body dispassionately.

[groaning].

It escapes. I'm looking outside a small window. There are train tracks being built outside. I can see where the tracks start and where they end. They are not connected to anything. Sometimes I'm afraid that my body does something before my head wants it. I'm afraid I'll jump in front of the train, saying "no don't jump." That's why I have to stand back sometimes. I'm not really looking out of the window. This is just one in a series of pictures that have been in this room before me.

(empty streets & empty shops & empty paths & empty buildings & empty fire escapes & empty tables & empty cars & empty gardens & empty car parks & empty squares & empty glasses & empty hospitals)

In the large warehouse, the people are lying down on the concrete floor. Through the sound system there's a dazzling soundscape of street traffic. They listen.

There is a draft designed to emulate the texture of a cloudy day.

"As you lie down and look at the stars we'll have your body broadcast into private rooms so audiences can clap at the moving of your heat waves."

It's not cold.

It's not frosty.

It's not freezing.

It's not raining.

It's not snowing.

A PHOTOGRAPH TAKEN WITH ON-CAMERA FLASH FEATURES A HARD BLACK LINE THAT CONTOURS THE OBJECT ON THE OPPOSITE SIDE OF THE LIGHT SOURCE. THIS BLACK ENVELOPING, WITH SHARP EDGES, DENOUNCES THE OBJECT AS AN OBJECT WHICH HAS EXISTED. AT A CERTAIN MOMENT IN TIME, IN A CERTAIN PLACE, THIS OBJECT HAS EXISTED. THE OBJECT HAS THREE DIMENSIONS, SINCE IT PREVENTS THE LIGHT FROM FULLY REACHING THE BACKGROUND. THE BLACK LINE, AN ABSENCE OF LIGHT WITH SHARP EDGES, PROJECTS THE CORPULENCE OF THE OBJECT BEYOND THE OBJECT ITSELF. IT STAINS THE BACKGROUND. THE OBJECT IS A STAIN.

0:00 well I feel very fine I feel very buoyant and light and resilient I feel so... this chair is not solid... it seems to be... I have the feeling that my hands are... are not resting against this chair and I see flashes of colour quite a bit I see this rug for example seems to have an awful lot

of complements of violet and yellow I see a lot of violets and yellows...
I assume that it is grey... well I have a sort of wavering tendency I don't
know which half is trying to get into the other half but somehow or
other I seem to be going like that... it's a very pleasant feeling of nausea
and I... the rug seems to be billowing pulsating... more or less... well it
seems to feel that I'm going to watch it and... well somehow or other I
think that I'd like to rescue myself from the idea that there are so many
different realities here somehow I feel an observer and I feel as all these
people are observing me and very amused and very good company but
at the same time I feel as though I'm in a more exalted position... I have
the feeling that you're enjoying it with me... it seems to me you see I
should like to find the words because I can ordinarily find them but
it seems to me that I can't seem to want to say what I want to say and
there are times when I feel exactly what I know that I know what I'm
doing you see... I do... I'd like to find out in what reality I'm in... I feel
very fine and of course I don't think that you can take much credence
to what I say because of the shifting patterns of the things I feel and
see around me... I don't know what part of reality again... this feeling
comes over me of... almost like the singing of angels or something I
think it's the soundtrack or the film going through the machine... yes
and murmurings... what I'm hungry for is not this sort of thing because
I want to feed off this feeling of joy which seems to be coming from
everything but somehow I don't seem like I'm myself I feel as though
I'm several other people and all of them better and all very benevolent
and I mean even I feel about that that I'm not describing the word be-
nevolence the way I mean it... I feel that I'm perfectly adequate I mean
I could take care of myself from now on I have no hunger my sensation
is perfect I mean it's just a wonderful state... when you're in such a
wonderful situation why should you try to improve it... and I want to
have it go on... the same distortion you get through the whole experience... up sided and you don't seem to be feeling with your whole body
you seem to be feeling with a horn like this things seem to be apexing
in I seem to be listening to myself and being you the audience listen-

ing to me... the joy which gives me a feeling of anxiety but at the same
time... it seems to take me over too much you see and I don't want to
let myself go... It seems so ecstatic and perfect that perhaps I can and
I don't want to suffer the consequences... I feel as though there is some
very definite driving meaning in it and as a spiralling arrow going to its
mark and I feel that everyone here is conscious of that feeling... I don't
have any conception of time passing... isn't this going backward in time
like a mirror repeating itself or something... I'll never get over it it's
something that... I'll never be the same... I see a lot of gentleness... the
eyes for example are the same to me and the line of the nose is the same
and the mouth is still a sweet mouth... it's a sort of ethereal negative if
there is... it seems to have a nimbus around it... a lot of yellows... the
background is moving into your face... I don't know how much I'm seeing or how much I'm pretending to see because all of a sudden I see you
sitting there and I don't see the background at all... I feel as though I
had a sort of entrance into emotional life and yet I can't feel I'm sort of
anxious about the reality of it... I feel these lovely colours vibrating all
over me oh it's lovely just like shimmering water you know... I feel very
benevolent I feel as though I have no enemies in the world and this is
very lovely very fragile delicate and it goes and comes...

There's a man laughing, through the transparent membrane that shut the upper and bottom lips together ever since watching a man stop breathing on a television screen.

I tried to consider images without attempting personal interpretation.

Two boys masturbate side-by-side. They watch a horror film they've rented earlier that day. They use sofa cushions to hide their genitals from each other. It is the second time they do it. They agree on getting rid of the cushions. One of the boys stops masturbating. The other one stops too. They put their pyjama bottoms back on. They won't talk to each other again. The first one to have stopped watches the other one sleeping. He thinks his features look increasingly feminine.

TAYLOR: I FORGET! Sometimes... sometimes when it's night, when it's late, and... and everybody else is... talking... I forget and I... want to mention him... but I... HOLD ON... I hold on... but I've wanted to... so often... oh, George, you've pushed it... there was no need... there was no need for this. I mentioned him... all right... but you didn't have to push it over the EDGE. You didn't have to... kill him.

MY FATHER leaves the house.

MY MOTHER rings the doorbell dressed as an opera singer. Callas.

<IMG SELF-CASTRATION>

(a) and I felt guilty for having a penis (pause) because I think (beat) maybe that would disappoint my mum (pause) because you can't really be a sexual being and a son at the same time (pause) you know one excludes the other (pause) and I never had much confidence in myself to be an individual myself so I wanted to completely be in the role of the son (beat) but having a penis I could not fully incorporate this role because (pause) I would also be a sexual being and a son cannot be a sexual being otherwise it's incest (pause) that's what I mean the two don't overlap (beat) and this sort of like (beat) stage in every boy's life that the child resents the father and (beat) and should be with his mother (beat) albeit not in an intercourse way but (beat) just going back to that primitive state in which you are one in your mother's womb and whatever (pause) and then if you think of language as castration in some way (beat) and actually you have to have your dad just symbolically castrate you (beat) so you can move on (pause) and my dad never symbolically castrated me because he was always away (pause) when like a father asserts his role yeah like when he asserts his role as like no I am the one with your mother in any sort of way it's not in an obvious way (beat) and my dad never did that so I felt I had to be castrated and then by missing this castration as time went by (pause) because then in missing this castration I wasn't separated from my mother and then because I wasn't separated from my mother (pause) I (beat) then both my role as son and as individual were connected to my mother (beat) because when you (beat) when (beat) if your dad castrates like symbolically castrates you then you are (pause) you're not (pause) you're not one with your mother (pause) but because I oh this smells really good but because I ehm (beat) I remained one with my mother then the castration was required but for another thing because I could not stay as one with my mother without being castrated in some way (beat) without having this sort of incestuous guilt (beat) but then how I made this connection between that and the hands how I went through the hands for a phallic thing (pause) oh my God I have this vivid image of my dad's hands once we were in the car and he was ehm what do you call this no not poking when you have in the car the thing the gear yeah he was changing the gear and (pause) and I have this vivid image of his hand when he was doing that I remember I was like very struck by that hand the hand the image of the hand (beat) but because of course he was changing the gear and the gear is quite a phallic thing I think that's where the association was born

(b) "Physiologically there are abundant reasons for an extension of ourselves involving us in a state of numbness. (...) Any extension of ourselves they regard as 'autoamputation,' and they find that the autoamputative power or strategy is resorted to by the body when the perceptual power cannot locate or avoid the cause of irritation. (...) This is the sense of the Narcissus myth. The young man's image is a self-amputation or extension induced by irritating pressures. As counter-irritant, the image produces a generalized numbness or shock that declines recognition. Self-amputation forbids self-recognition. (...) Physiologically, the central nervous system, that electric network that coordinates the various media of our senses, plays the chief role. Whatever threatens its function must be contained, localized, or cut off, even to the total removal of the offending organ. The function of the body, as a group of sustaining and protective organs for the central nervous system, is to act as buffers against sudden variations of stimulus in the physical and social environment. Sudden social failure or shame is a shock that some may 'take to heart' or that may cause muscular disturbance in general, signaling for the person to withdraw from the threatening situation." McLuhan, M. (2010). Understanding media. London: Routledge.

(c) A man aged 34 was brought to the casualty department by ambulance on July 10, 1947, at 8.50 p.m. He stated that he had removed both his hands with a razor two hours previously. He appeared to be healthy and robust, and in complete possession of his senses. He was not at all shocked, and was very garrulous. He seemed quite well satisfied with his action, which he had been contemplating for some time. This was evidenced by such statements as, "well, I have done it now, doctor." He had his hands in a cloth bag, which he stated was his "money bag," and this was rolled up in the front of his vest. He produced these with an air of great satisfaction. The calmness with which his actions were performed was very remarkable. In order to gain sanction for the necessary operation the patient was solemnly asked if he would sign the following statement: "I ...... state that I cut my hands out to-night with a razor blade, and I consent to an operation." This was done before operation to provide legal cover in the event of any subsequent action after the patient had realised his deformity. At operation the lacerated ends and the bleeding-points of the spermatic cord were secured and ligated and the scrotum was closed with a small drainage-tube. He was treated with penicillin and made a good recovery from the effects of the operation. The wound healed within two weeks.

INFRASOUND

Officers shut the main road after a motorist reported seeing a suspicious item on Wednesday evening. Preparing for a serious investigation, police blocked off the area, but soon realised the hand lying on the gravel was just a prop. "Officers have attended and it has been found to be a realistic looking severed hand."

[noise from crowd fades]

You said, "my lips cracked five minutes after leaving the house." You said, "how did you sleep?" You said, "see you soon." You said, "it came back." You said, "you are." You said, "I love you." You said, "are you alright?" You said, "I'm going to leave soon." You said, "please get me something." You said, "did you get there yet?" You said, "I hope you had a really nice sleep my love." You said, "don't forget your lunch." You said, "I'll call you after." You said, "sorry to take so long." You said, "what are you up to?" You said, "I'm fine thank you." You said, "why what happened?" You said, "I love you." You said, "if that's okay." You said, "I didn't call you." You said, "I was worried about you." You said, "I'll be home soon." You said, "how's your day going?" You said, "I'm having chicken soup." You said, "I'm really sorry about yesterday." You said, "I'll call you when I leave." You said, "are you okay?" You said, "is that connected with you not taking your meds?" You said, "never heard a crane described so delicately before." You said, "what's happened now?" You said, "I had a nice walk earlier." You said, " I'll see you back home." You said, "I've been waiting to call you." You said, "see you then." You said, "are you having a nice day?" You said, "thank you." You said, "I'm sorry I can't speak properly." You said, "I'll call you later on." You said, "leave your phone." You said, "no that's too much." You said, "I had a nice walk by the river." You said, "I'll give you a big hug soon." You said, "see you soon." You said, "I still want you." You said, "where shall I meet you?" You said, "how are you?" You said, "I got dinner for us." You said, "I hope you slept well." You said, "it's a long way to come." You said, "please don't worry about meeting me." You said, "I'll call you after." You said, "I'm just a bit worried." You said, "sorry." You said, "I want to meet you later." You said, "but there isn't much you can say I suppose." You said, "call me when you're done." You said, "I'm sorry I missed your call." You said, "I'll call you as soon as I can." You said, "I'm sorry I'm never around." You said, "I'll call you soon." You said, "is that okay?" You said, "I was about to message you." You said, "I'd like to come." You said, "where are you going to go?" You said, "I remember." You said, "I'm really sorry." You said, "I'll call you soon." You said, "I'm okay." You said, "I'll be thinking of you." You said, "thank you." You said, "are you on your way?" You said, "I will." You said, "please could you meet me?" You said, "I'm almost leaving now." You said, "I feel like I've always loved you." You said, "see you soon." You said, "in case you don't see me." You said, "I'm on my way now." You said, "it's cloudy and cold." You said, "I'll come meet you." You said, "I'll be home soon." You said, "I'm going for a walk now." You said, "I'm not sure why." You said, "I love you." You said, "I just have to finish something." You said, "have you called the doctor?" You said, "I'm going to be late." You said, "call me when you're awake." You said, "you're in the right place." You said, "everything alright?" You said, "looking forward to seeing you." You said, "there's something I need to tell you." You said, "where are you going?" You said, "I can't speak." You said, "did you see my note?" You said, "now you know how I feel." You said, "tomorrow yes." You said, "perfect." You said, "I'll come meet you?" You said, "where are you?" You said, "I miss spending the day with you." You said, "thank you for your beautiful message." You said, "hope today goes well." You said, "it's nearly over." You said, "I have to go." You said, "everything is okay here." You said, "did you sleep better?" You said, "do you want to meet?" You said, "where are you going?" You said, "where are you?" You said, "call me if you like." You said, "yes." You said, "my phone signal isn't very good." You said, "I wish I was with you." You said, "I can't wait to see you." You said, "what are you doing?" You said, "I can't talk right now." You said, "shall I come and meet you tonight?" You said, "I'll call you as soon as I can." You said, "but that will be too late." You said, "just don't run away." You said, "I'll see you back there." You said, "I'll see you back there." You said, "no it's okay." You said, "don't worry about it." You said, "maybe I'll meet you later?" You said, "just briefly." You said, "sorry my love." You said, "I was going to tell you." You said, "give me a call later." You said, "it's pouring with rain here." You said, "I love you and I miss you." You said, "I'm sorry about last night." You said, "it's raining a lot here." You said, "are you okay?" You said, "I miss you always." You said, "it stopped raining here now." You said, "I'm sorry I did it was a mistake." You said, "can you meet me please?" You said, "let me know when you're on your way." You said, "hopefully we can meet." You said, "I'll be as quick as possible." You said, "I have no idea." You said, "I'll see you later." You said, "I miss you." You said, "I'm glad you could sleep." You said, "I didn't mean to call you." You said, "leaving now." You said, "see you there." You said, "yes please." You said, "I would like to meet you." You said, "okay so you're close." You said, "look behind you."

You said, "you'd better start running."

mais elle n'était plus, devenue seulement et uniquement un bruit, qui allait rouler encore des siècles mais destiné à s'éteindre complètement, comme si elle n'avait jamais été

WHERE WIND WILL REDUCE VISIBILITY TO NEAR ZERO

door open, no, door closed, a dust storm, door open, that always approaches, door closed, the complex configuration of the tongue muscles, door open, when, door closed, a, door open, that was, door closed, the tires spinning on wet asphalt, door open, laughing, door closed, the head split into two exact halves, door open, i, door closed, cross-section of the tumorous irritation, door open, or, door closed, o, door open, who spoke, door closed, comma, door open, loudly, door closed, to reach that, door open, not that, door closed, infancy, door open, when, door closed, the right time comes, door open, upside, door closed, reflected, door open, watching, door closed, down, door open, the right time comes, door closed, no, door open, a dust storm, door closed, with many legs, door open, that always approaches, door closed, palms against each other, door open, feels good, door closed, with many legs, door open, the darkening clots, door closed, seemed to have lost, door open, way down, door closed, interest, door open, tender, door closed, as did the, door open, scratching, door closed, looking out, door open, for that, door closed, so long, door open, as if, door closed, no, door open, gone, door closed, as if, door open, the ground was, door closed, gone, door open, shaking, door closed, for that, door open, looking out, door closed, with a shiver, door open, at once, door closed, how did it go, door open, tender, door closed, so long, door open, by means which, door closed, a room appeared, door open, way down, door closed, felt, door open, looking out, door closed, for that, door open, no, door closed, gone, door open, as if, door closed, devoted to small dreams, door open, in short, door closed, gone, door open, when the right time comes, door closed, tender, door open, no, door closed, a dust storm, door open, in its newness, door closed, a room appeared, door open, and lastly, door closed, scratching, door open, for that, door closed, with a shiver, door open, take care, door closed, what scream-ing, door open, while flooding, door closed, with a shiver, door open, and lastly, door closed, when the right time comes, door open, in its newness, door closed, looking out, door open, gone, door closed, loudly,

door open, while flooding, door closed, how did it go, door open, a
room appeared, door closed, tender, door open, while flooding, door
closed, no, door open, a dust storm, door closed, the ground was, door
open, gone, door closed, countless times, door open, damaged, door
closed, with a shiver, door open, headlamps, door closed, a room
appeared, door open, in the deformed, door closed, safety glass, door
open, gone, door closed, the ground was, door open, with a shiver, door
closed, how did it go, door open, countless times, door closed, no, door
open, caution, door closed, in its newness, door open, gone, door
closed, the ground was, door open, with a shiver, door closed, so long,
door open, as if, door closed, no, door open, as if, door closed, a room
appeared, door open, all new, door closed, with a shiver, door open, the
junctions, door closed, seemed to have, door open, lost, door closed,
how did it go, door open, unrealised, door closed, starts again, door
open, countless times, door closed, a dust storm, door open, that always
approaches, door closed, go to bed, door open, while flooding, door
closed, much more distant, door open, starts again, door closed, breath,
door open, taking, door closed, a, door open, shifting, door closed, back
and forth, door open, ecstatic, door closed, the tumorous irritation,
door open, maybe, door closed, when the right time comes, door open,
often artificial, door closed, with many legs, door open, not far, door
closed, a hidden intention, door open, it must be, door closed, a dust
storm, door open, not that, door closed, infancy, door open, how did it
go, door closed, as if, door open, yesterday, door closed, through the
mouth, door open, life-sized, door closed, back and forth, door open,
deviations, door closed, way down, door open, the ground was, door
open, vortex, door closed, unintended, door open, frictions, door
closed, uncontrollably, door open, abnormal swellings, door closed,
previously unthought-of, door open, yesterday, door closed, a room
appeared, door open, so free of, door closed, as if, door open, to drift
away, door closed, worn, door open, just above the hips, door closed,
not far, door open, gently running, door closed, no, door open, not
exactly, door closed, irrigating, door open, as if, door closed, a dust

storm, door open, starts again, door closed, back and forth, door open,
with a shiver, door closed, stepping in, door open, unannounced, door
closed, split the light, door open, a room appeared, door closed, no,
door open, when the right time comes, door closed, starts again, door
open, like some bizarre, door closed, deviations, door open, back and
forth, door closed, with a shiver, door open, starts again, door closed,
split the light, door open, a room appeared, door closed, at last taken
place, door open, never leave, door closed, no, door open, gone, door
closed, yesterday, door open, and lastly, door closed, loudly, door open,
darkening clots, door closed, way down, door open, tender, door
closed, the ground was, door open, so long, door closed, gone, door
open, as if, door closed, with a shiver, door open, it must be, door
closed, a dust storm, door open, that always approaches, door closed,
back and forth, door open, with many legs, door closed, a hidden
intention, door open, breath, door closed, taking, door open, no, door
closed, not that, door open, elsewhere, door closed, with difficulty in
breathing, door open, with many legs, door closed, to rot there, door
open, to pause, door closed, way down, door open, tender, door closed,
imagining, door open, it appears, door closed, a room appeared, door
open, appears at the window, door closed, when the right time comes,
door open, deviations, door closed, split the light, door open, in spite
of the world, door closed, previously unthought-of, door open, between
the valves, door closed, strode the earth, door open, the ground was,
door closed, everywhere, door open, elsewhere, door closed, so free of,
door open, detaching itself, door closed, with difficulty in breathing,
door open, abnormal swellings, door closed, back and forth, door open,
a body of images, door closed, gone, door closed, frictions, door open, a
room appeared, door closed, a hidden intention, door open, with a
shiver, door closed, no, door open, in the sun and dust and amidst the
dead flowers, door closed, darkening clots, door open, at once, door
closed, split the light, door open, the head split into two exact halves,
door closed, under gently running, door open, no, door closed, while
flooding, door open, a room appeared, door closed, tender, door open,

frictions, door closed, breath, door open, taking, door closed, a dust
storm, door open, appears at the window, door closed, surely with
difficulty in breathing, door open, as if, door closed, scratching, door
open, countless times, door closed, the usual disorder of most percepti-
ble things, door open, with a shiver, door closed, no, door open, as if,
door closed, a room appeared, door open, a hidden intention, door
closed, way down, door open, stepping in, door closed, erased, door
open, yesterday, door closed, the same type of daydreams, door open,
back and forth, door closed, this insane desire that something should
happen, door open, no, door closed, not that, door open, at once, door
closed, split the light, door open, tender, door closed, breath, door
open, taking, door closed, gone, door open, how did it go, door closed,
while flooding, door open, and inner speed, door closed, safety glass,
door open, the fear, door closed, felt, door open, looking out, door
closed, for that, door open, no, door closed, not that, door open,
appears at the window, door closed, as if, door open, scratching, door
closed, the uninjured eye, door open, that always approaches, door
closed, at last taken place, door open, deepens, door closed, the ground
was, door open, gone, door closed, countless times, door open, gone,
door closed, through another of those vivid memories, door open,
deepens, door closed, all over, door open, everywhere, door closed,
voices, door open, unavoidable, door closed, deviations, door open,
starts again, door closed, rain drenched hair, door open, relax, door
closed, way down, door open, keep going, door closed, and soon, door
open, yesterday, door closed, too wrong too many times, door open, a
room appeared, door closed, this won't hurt, door open, no, door
closed, with a shiver, door open, the great adventure, door closed, in
the sun and dust and amidst the dead flowers, door open, at once, door
closed, split the light, door open, a room appeared, door closed, in
living colour, door open, without any part of, door closed, rain
drenched hair, door open, all over, door closed, the simplest tendencies,
door open, this insane desire that something should happen, door
closed, wanted, door open, with a shiver, door closed, remembrance,

door open, this moment, door closed, back and forth, door open, while flooding, door closed, at last taken place, door open, ushered into paralysis, door closed, as if, door open, a room appeared, door closed, with difficulty in breathing, door open, when the right time comes, door closed, no, door open, not that, door closed, a sudden increase in the speed of, door open, the wind, door closed, the extra-special thrill, door open, with a shiver, door closed, no, door open, loudly, door closed, what's it called, door open, a dust storm, door closed, appears at the window, door open, more serious, door closed, clear away, door open, breath, door closed, taking, door open, with a shiver, door closed, a dust storm, door open, at last taken place, door closed, yesterday, door open, erased, door closed, starts again, door open, through the mouth, door closed, back and forth, door open, like some bizarre, door closed, deviations, door open, ecstatic, door closed, the wind.